Echoes

A Novel by
CLIFTON LABREE

Published by
Fading Shadows Imprint
New Boston, New Hampshire, USA

ISBN-10: 1-943329-23-0
ISBN-13: 978-1-943329-23-6

Cover Design by Vivian LaBree

Dedicated to my wife Pauline, and my family, with thanks for all their support and encouragement.

Chapter One

The hospital ward was dark except for a desk lamp illuminating the nurse's duty station beside the entrance door. Most of the wounded soldiers were sleeping. Colonel Troy Hansen stared at the ceiling thankful for the veil of darkness that hid the tears beginning to well in his deep-set eyes. Memories of the men he had sent into battle haunted him. Some of the young soldiers were barely out of high school with a long future and promises of great things to look forward to. Now they belonged to the legions of forever young. He saw their faces everywhere. They had looked up to him and trusted his ability to lead them in battle.

Forty-eight hours ago he was at the head of his infantry regiment in an assault against a heavily fortified North Vietnamese Army installation beside the Mekong River. The day was hot and humid. The air was saturated with the smell of cordite and gun powder from the supporting batteries of artillery and the putrid aroma of human feces from the nearby rice paddies. It was impossible to by-pass or out flank the enemy, so Colonel Hansen ordered all three of his battalions into a frontal attack. Losses were greater than expected, but the position was overrun. He recalled seeing several of his young soldiers lying together where they had been hit by mortar fire. They were partially imbedded in the soft mud with their arms stretched out in front of them, almost as if they were resting. Closer examination revealed bloody entrails covering the ground around them. Their eyes were still open registering the horror and disbelief of what was happening to them. He had curtly ordered the bodies covered and turned away to retch. The grisly images returned with increased frequency and vividness.

1

Colonel Hansen was one of the last casualties. When his unit was in the combat zone he was always up front where he could see what was going on. It was beginning to get dark, and he was reconnoitering the positioning of outposts for the night when an enemy machine gun ripped through the stillness of the battlefield. All he remembered was that the blast momentarily lifted him off the ground. The reality of being hit made him angry. His left leg was shattered and several bullets had entered his upper body cavity. Within minutes a helicopter had plucked him from the battlefield and rushed him to a field hospital which stopped the flow of blood from his violated body.

Luck was with him. The bullets were destructive, but they missed his heart and spinal column. A broken rib, a severed spleen and a minor rupture of his lungs constituted the sum of his internal injuries. His left leg was broken in several places, and would probably end his military career.

The tall well-built Colonel, with specks of gray in his sandy hair, had always been proud of the way he carried out missions assigned to the units he had commanded throughout his career in the Army. He was a three-war veteran of World War II, Korea, and Vietnam. His greatest losses in a single day took place the same day he was wounded. Forty percent of his regiment was wiped out. It was twenty times more than were in his graduating class at the small town in Maine where he grew up. He could not accept the magnitude of the tragedy and felt responsible. Hundreds of families were going to be torn asunder when the devastating messages of death arrived to shatter the tranquility of the home.

Even when he was under the influence of pain killers and sedatives, he was reviewing what he had done in that long day of battle that might have caused the heavy losses. Young soldiers fresh out of boot camp had displayed an eagerness and a tenacity to close with the enemy. They had followed him into the death trap with complete trust in his leadership. Their contorted faces were now driving him crazy. They were his responsibility and he had lost them for a foul smelling piece of barren real estate. The duty nurse passed his bed and saw the tear stains on his clean pillow. She placed a comforting hand on his arm.

"Are you all right, Colonel?" she asked in a hushed voice.

Troy shook his head. There was nothing she nor medical science could do to cure the pain he carried. "Thank you, nurse," he answered in a slurred voice. His tongue felt twice as large as normal. "I lost over four hundred men in one day! What can I say to their families who entrusted them to my care?"

"Would you like a stronger sedative? The doctors have authorized it if needed."

"No," Troy answered quickly, turning away from the nurse. "Where am I?"

"You were taken from the battlefield to a field surgical center where your wounds were evaluated and treated. Then you were flown to this hospital ship where we've double checked your condition. Corrective surgery has been completed on your body wounds. You're a lucky soldier. In time you'll recover without any long-range limitations. Your leg will require additional surgery in the future. The doctors can explain that to you in the morning. Right now you should be glad that you still have it."

"Thank you, nurse..." Troy fell asleep in mid-sentence. The nurse took his pulse and wiped beads of sweat from his forehead. The smell of disinfectant permeated the ward. His state of consciousness between normal sleep and medicine-induced slumber began to wander.

* * *

Troy's mind returned to another hospital ship, years ago, off the coast of Italy. It was January, 1944. Over the years he had frequently visited the memory with sharp clarity and detail. Furious battles were still raging on the Italian Peninsula where he had been wounded in the shoulder by a German sniper bullet that broke his collar bone and injured several of his arm muscles. He had awoke from anesthesia and asked the same question of a nurse near his bunk. He was frightened at first.

"Where am I?" he had cried on the verge of hysterics.

"You're on a hospital ship in the Mediterranean, Lieutenant," answered the nurse in a calm soothing voice. Her soft fingers sent shivers through his body as she felt for his pulse. Her light blond hair was pulled back behind her ears fastened with a barrette. She wore a Naval Nurse headband with an ensign bar attached. She filled the room with a serene optimism felt by all of the wounded men in her care. "You're going to get a break from combat for a few weeks, Lieutenant Hansen. Your arm and shoulder are broken and it looks as if you'll be in our care for a while."

"I thought I was going to an Army hospital."

"They transported you to the Navy. Most of the wounded on the ship are Army. The Navy is fighting the war too, Lieutenant," she remarked with a smile.

Troy's traction bed was elevated more than the other bunks allowing him unrestricted view of the ward. He could feel the gentle rocking motion of the ship. That first night on board, he observed a patient being attended by the same nurse that had spoken to him. She was bent over the stricken soldier whispering something in his ear. There was a sad forlorn look in her eyes. Her voice had an angelic quality that was comforting. She administered medicine into the plastic tubes sticking out of the soldier's arms, assuring him that she was with him.

The scene was forever etched on Troy's soul. The angel of mercy remained at the soldier's side for hours until life no longer existed in his shattered body. She gently closed his gaping eyelids, covered his face with the white sheet, and stood motionless over the inert body, weeping for several minutes. Troy heard nothing in the stillness of the ward, but he saw the convulsive sobs that wracked the nurse's body.

The dedicated nurse had won the hearts and admiration of every wounded man. She was indefatigable, rarely leaving the ward. Later, after they had become better acquainted, Troy had asked her how she stood up to such ordeals day after day. Her reply was simple and eloquent:

"When I completed nursing school, I could never have imagined so much human suffering and tragedy as I've experienced on this ship. Yet, in the presence of all that pain and misery, I saw gallantry, compassion, and unselfishness on an unprecedented scale. The wounded are considerate and understanding of the others in the wards. They've shown me how fragile the human body really is and that the human spirit cannot be defeated. The most precious treasure that exists in the wards of the wounded men is that of hope. Hope for a better tomorrow, and hope that all is not lost. I consider it a privilege to serve such men."

Ensign Gail Malone was not an easy person to forget. That had been twenty-five years ago. He could still hear her voice, and recall the sadness that had filled her green eyes as they said good-bye, standing beneath a dimly lit lamppost in a small English village near the coast. The hurt returned just as acute as it did the first time he learned that their parting had been a final one. A portion of him was still with the gentle nurse he had fallen in love with and never saw again!

Images from the past were as vivid now as the day they had taken place. Troy lost himself in their comforting warmth as often as he could. His wounds from the Italian campaign were a long time in healing. He had stayed on the hospital ship for a month until the cast was removed. During that time the ship sailed for England where it was undergoing a refitting in preparation for the coming assault of Fortress Europe across the English Channel. By the time the Naval hospital ship docked at Portsmouth, Troy and Ensign Malone had become friends.

Troy was assigned to a physical therapy center near Portsmouth on the Channel coast where his arm was manipulated and massaged until it returned to normal. Gail was transferred from the ship and temporarily assigned to an Army hospital staff nearby.

They saw each other occasionally. Troy had worked up the courage to ask her for a date, and she accepted. Dressed in his best uniform Troy could recall every moment of that first evening. On his right breast he wore the battle ribbons he had won. Above them he placed his most cherished adornment – the Combat Infantryman's Badge. It had the picture of a long Kentucky muzzleloader rifle against a blue background. It was awarded only to those soldiers who had fought in a major battle. It added ten dollars a month to his paycheck, which was welcome, but more than anything else it was a symbol of his rites of passage, and a ticket to the combat brotherhood fraternity. He was proud of the membership.

They went to the Officer's Club for dinner. The Lounge was crowded and boisterous. The dining section was relatively quiet and sparsely populated. Up to that time, Troy had only seen Gail dressed in everyday white uniforms. That first date she wore her Navy blue uniform with a dark blue cape over her shoulders. Her eyes lit up when she smiled. She was a vision of loveliness.

"I can't believe that you're the same nurse I've been watching for weeks in the ship's ward," exclaimed Troy. "You're beautiful, Ensign."

"Thank you, Lieutenant," she acknowledged with modest grace. "You look better in that uniform than you do in a hospital Johnnie."

"I feel better too," laughed Troy, offering her his left arm. His right arm was still supported with a sling.

That first evening he learned that she had been engaged to a Navy Captain who was lost at sea when his ship was torpedoed in the North Atlantic, an early victim of the war. Her situation was not unique. It was an uncertain period when no relationship was permanent. Dreams and plans of thousands of young men and women were placed on hold until the war was over. The war influenced every aspect of people's lives. Fear and the pain of loss were emotions that everybody lived with. Men and women in uniform dealt with their mortality in different ways. Troy had developed a "what-the-hell" attitude after his baptism of combat. He was no longer afraid of dying, accepting it as a part of being a soldier. The death of his men was a different matter. He never forgot.

There was a nervous energy in the air. Troy and Gail knew that he would soon be assigned to a rifle company being formed in England as a part of the massive force about to be hurled against the German-occupied French coast.

Troy had shared some of his childhood experiences growing up in a small town in northern Maine with Gail. Most of the people worked hard trying to provide for a family. His father had struggled to feed and clothe them during the depression. Work was scarce, and every man in town vied for any job that became available. His dad had a reputation of being reliable and diligent. The local road agent stopped at their house a few times a month to offer him a day or two working on the roads when his budget allowed the expenditure. When that took place, the family rejoiced at their good fortune.

Large gardens, called "Victory Gardens" were a mainstay for the average family. Troy laughed with Gail, telling her that it always seemed to need weeding. He had hated it and was determined to do something with his life besides being a farmer, but he did like working on the family woodlot cutting firewood for the two stoves in their house and for his elderly grandmother who lived nearby. He was the younger of two brothers, graduating from the University of Maine in Orono with a major in military science and education. He was in his last year at school when Pearl Harbor was bombed, December 7, 1941. He had completed the requirements necessary for the degrees and joined the Army immediately after the war began. His brother was killed during the first year of the war.

"Don't you yearn to be back there now?" asked Gail, sipping her cup of tea. She was a good listener and Troy was embarrassed that he was talking too much about himself.

"Oh yes," replied Troy. "It seems so far away and long ago. It was another world and I'm afraid that when this war is over that world we once knew will never exist again."

"With all the destruction and misery taking place it's hard to imagine that anything can remain as it was," Gail reflected. "I was apprehensive when I joined the Navy directly out of nursing school. Now, I'm frightened for what the future holds. Many of my nurse friends feel the same way."

Troy watched Gail. She was a private person of many moods. The depths of her feelings could be observed when she was caring for those who needed her healing touch, and she was more in control. Beyond the ward, in the Officer's Club, she was less certain of herself. She had seen a lot of pain inflicted by the war and it showed in her sad eyes. She had been observing Troy closely all evening. When their eyes met she was quick to break contact. She told him that she too was a New Englander from Buzzard's Bay, Massachusetts on Cape Cod.

"We're practically neighbors," she smiled. "I was the only girl in our family. I have two brothers. One was killed in North Africa. The other is in the North Atlantic with the Coast Guard."

"I'm sorry, Ensign. We share losses. I lost a brother in the Army Air Corps. He was shot down over Germany."

"Sometimes I think that I'm the only one to feel the way I do, but death and grief are common throughout the land. No one is immune to the terrifying encounter," Gail noted solemnly.

The music from the lounge and dance floor penetrated the dining room. "If I didn't have this sling on my right arm, I'd ask you to dance. I was never very good at it, but I'd try."

The soft strains of *I'll Be Seeing You In All The Old Familiar Places,* filtered through the Club. It was a favorite of the British and Americans. The mood changed in an instant and the Club was quiet and pensive. The song never failed to touch everyone's heart.

"If you're willing, we could try it. We'll never know unless we do," she suggested, listening to the sad refrain.

"Okay, I'll try not to step on your polished shoes," answered Troy, offering her a hand. He placed his left hand in her right. She grasped him around the waist with her left arm. They danced several sets of slow waltzes and fox-trots. The music was soothing and melancholic. They enjoyed the intimate interlude. She came up to his chin. Troy detected the subtle aroma of perfume. She clung firmly to him but allowed him to lead as she followed him across the dance floor. There was a vitality and freshness to her that was intoxicating. He knew that first night that he was in love with her. Later, he had escorted her to nurse's quarters. They were silent and reflective as they walked arm and arm down the rows of metal Quonset huts.

"It has been swell being with you," Troy said, reluctant for the evening to end. "I'd like to see you again if it's possible."

"It has been nice, Troy," she answered, using his name for the first time. "One of my roommates works at the therapy center so I can relay my schedule to you through her."

"That would be great. Goodnight, Gail. Until next time." He reached out to embrace her with his left arm.

She lifted her lips to him. "Goodnight, Troy."

Even now, twenty-five years later, he could feel their softness and the contentment that had filled his heart.

Chapter Two

"Colonel Hansen," announced an orderly standing over Troy's bed. "Are you Colonel Troy Hansen?"

Troy slowly opened his eyes and looked at the orderly. "Yes," he said groggily. "I hope you haven't woke me up to give me a sleeping pill."

"Of course not, Sir. You have some Army visitors and we're holding the ship's departure until they return to shore. Shall I bring them in, Sir?"

"Yes, if it's not against regulations."

A few minutes later, Troy was sitting up in bed drinking ginger ale with a tray across his lap. His visitors included a Brigadier General Holland the brigade commander, a couple of the battalion commanders and several enlisted men from his regiment. They quietly gathered around his bed so that he could see them.

"Colonel Hansen," said General Holland. "I know that they just woke you from a sound sleep, and I apologize for the intrusion. I've spoken to the head doctor aboard and he tells me that you're doing better than expected."

"They've told me the same thing, General," Troy replied. "Thanks for coming. I appreciate the visit. I can tell you guys that never in my career have I commanded a better group of men. I'm proud of your performance. I apologize for losing so many of your buddies."

"I understand your feelings, Colonel," said General Holland. "We won't take up any more time, but those of us who could break away from the division wanted to board the ship to tell you how much we appreciated the way you looked after the men. You may find some relief in the fact that your courageous assault on the hill made it possible for us to retrieve several outfits that had been surrounded and isolated by observed enemy artillery fire. You removed that observation position. Headquarters has authorized the Distinguished Service Cross be awarded to you for valorous leadership under enemy fire. We salute you, Colonel Hansen." The burly General attached the medal to a pillow next to Troy's head and left the ward.

Each of the men presented themselves so that Troy recognized them through the mist covering his eyes. All he could say was a weak "Thank you…"

The ship's head doctor had witnessed the presentation and added his congratulations to the proud Colonel. "It's been a privilege to witness the scene, Colonel. From the things several of the men told me, the medal is richly deserved. I want to let you know that the ship is pulling anchor and heading to Pearl Harbor where you'll be transferred to the Army hospital at Schofield Barracks."

"That will be great, Doctor."

Several days after the medal presentation, nurses helped Troy get in a wheel chair with one leg stirrup held straight to support his leg. They wheeled him out on the warm sunny deck. It felt good to be free of the ward. His spirits increased as he watched the sun reflect on the water and felt the cool breeze against his face.

The ponderous hospital ship rode easily in the gentle swells of the South China Sea. Two Coast guard Cutters escorted the ship, one on each side. They were beautiful vessels. They reminded Troy of wild mustangs prancing about ready to leap to wherever they were needed. He spent all day on the deck. It exhausted him, but the change in routine helped him sleep better that night. The further the ship steamed from Vietnam, the more relaxed he became. The solitude of the night at sea allowed him to revisit those moments of the past that held him hostage.

As long as Troy and Gail were still in England, they were able to see each other occasionally. Sometimes they went to a movie in the small village and, occasionally, they attended special USO shows that toured the numerous Army camps.

Those moments together were highlights of their existence. Gail spent twelve to fourteen hours on her shifts at the medical complex being established in England by the Army and Navy. It was an exhausting routine. The quiet periods she spent with Troy were an oasis of calm and peace in the center of organized chaos. Both knew that something special was taking place between them. Within the highly tense atmosphere it was not easy to think of the future, for it had a way of being shaped by the destructive forces that surrounded them. Nothing was absolute or permanent, uncertainty prevailed!

One warm, sunny day in May, they were able to get away for twenty-four hours. They rented bicycles and rode across the bridge from the mainland to the Isle of Wright. It was a heavily fortified piece of land filled with large-bore coastal batteries and anti-aircraft guns. Troy had brought along a couple of army C-rations and a small bottle of wine for the occasion. They had a picnic on a relatively isolated seawall on the shore. The tide was out and the water was calm for the Channel. Visibility was clear enough that they could see some of the Cherbourg Peninsula due south of Wright. Being able to see enemy-held land was unsettling. A small body of water was all that separated the two combatant nations.

Gail was dressed in her blue uniform with a long coat. It could be cool along the shore and she brought along a small thermos of tea and started to pour two cups.

"I didn't like tea when I was younger, now, I like it better," she remarked, passing a small cup to Troy.

"I like it, but coffee is still my favorite. I thought the Navy operated on coffee?" Troy kidded her.

"Well maybe they do," she laughed with him. She had a way of tilting her head slightly to the left when she expressed herself. "You know, I may be attached to the Army for a while longer. The ship is still in dry-dock. There's a large contingent of Navy personnel attached to the medical complex."

"I've seen them at the therapy center too. My shoulder is fine now. I've been assigned to a company being formed in England. I brought along something," announced Troy, holding a set of captain bars in his hand. "Would you do me the honor of pinning them on me?"

12

"Oh, my, Troy. I'm so proud of you," she exclaimed, accepting the insignias. She attached them to his shoulder straps, placing his first lieutenant silver bars in her pocket. "May I have them for a souvenir?"

"Sure if you want them," he replied.

Gail placed her arms around him and held on tightly. The ominous presence of the Cherbourg landfall erased the warmth she had felt a moment before.

"I never thought I could feel this way again. I'm afraid to be happy because anything can happen to take it away. I'm frightened of the future, Troy. I don't know if I can hold out until the end. The worst is yet to come," she cried with trembling lips.

"I know Gail. I know," he answered in a whisper. He had similar thoughts, but he kept them to himself. "We can draw courage from the fact that everyone else is going through the same thing." He kissed her on the forehead and held her close.

"Surely what we have between us is real," she said softly. "Yet, reality is also that piece of land across the water... I can't imagine all the strife that is going to take place when we start the invasion."

"Come now, Gail. Don't dwell on the negatives," Troy had tried to comfort her. "If we listen to our hopes and dreams for the future, it will make it easier for us to carry out our duties whatever they are."

"What are you trying to say, Troy?"

"May I make a date with you at a time and place back home after the war? Maybe six months after Germany is defeated. We should be back in the states by then. You live in Massachusetts and I live in Maine. How about if we select a place in New Hampshire between the two?"

"That sounds exciting. Where would be a good place to set our rendezvous?" she added.

"I've been around the Portsmouth area some. A friend of mine was stationed at a coastal battery at Odiorne Point in Newcastle," he had casually mentioned.

"I went to the Wentworth-By-The-sea Hotel in Newcastle for a wedding reception a few years ago. It was beautiful. We could meet on the large porch at the main entrance."

"Sounds great," Troy answered, releasing her to retrieve a small notepad and a stubby pencil from his tunic pocket. "We agree that it will be exactly one hundred and eighty days after the surrender of Germany. I'll make two copies of the date so that we won't be confused. If it's impossible to make the date and we are out of touch, we could call the desk to leave a message."

Troy added their two home addresses to the notes and passed one to her. They sealed the date with a kiss. The balance of the day they pedaled to a small inn near the coastline where they had reserved two rooms. They dined in an ancient tavern warmed by a crackling fireplace. It took up one whole side of the room. Gail's mood had improved from earlier in the day. After a hearty meal they lingered over wine. Gail had laughed that, in an emergency, the C-rations were okay, but she preferred a regular cooked meal like she got on the ship. Troy nodded his head in approval.

It was a day in which they acknowledged their feelings for each other, and committed themselves to the future as much as it was possible during those unsettling war years. They left the dining room and climbed the narrow twisting stairs to their adjoining rooms. Troy kissed her outside the door to her room.

"I don't want to be alone tonight," she confided softly in his ear.

"Neither do I."

That night the love they had discovered for each other was shared and they became one. A bond of trust and love had been formed that would sustain them for the dark ordeal that had to be dealt with before they could be together again. Their love nurtured the hope they shared for the future.

The next morning the room was filled with the soft scent of lilacs. Large bunches of lilacs with blooming flowers grew beneath the bedroom windows of the inn. It was an aroma that Troy would always associate with Gail and the night they had spent together. It was a high point of their relationship and the last time they were able to spend more than a couple of hours together. Available time for private affairs was a scarce commodity.

14

Gail had told Troy that last evening she was going to accompany the Army's field hospital battalion to France when the invasion began and passed on to him the mailing address of the unit. They promised to write as often as possible.

Twenty-five years later, Troy was astounded at the clarity of his recollection of that last time they saw each other. They knew that the invasion was imminent and that they would be a part of the first troops ashore. They tried to put on a cheerful face for each other, but parting was difficult. Neither knew if it was the end of an era or the beginning of the future. The unknown was the most frightening element of the war. It permeated every person's thoughts and deeds.

They had waited for their respective buses to return to base beneath the dimly lit lamp post near the Canteen entrance. It was a foggy and damp night. Warm clothes felt good. A chill ran up and down Gail's spine making her shiver in the cool air. They clung to each other with a silent desperation. Pledging to keep in touch regardless of where the war took them. It was a tearful parting. Gail's bus came first. He helped her climb aboard. She turned on the steps and looked at him with tears streaming down her cheeks. With a wave of her hand and a silent good-bye she disappeared from view.

Troy stood beneath the lamppost consumed with loneliness. In his heart he had a haunting premonition that he was never going to see Gail again. He felt like running after the bus and taking her away somewhere so that the war could not separate them. He turned from the light and wept, feeling empty, abandoned, and helpless that the gentle nurse he had fallen in love with was going to war again, and there was nothing he could do to protect her. He boarded the bus back to base with a heavy heart and a fervent prayer that a benevolent God would watch over her.

The D-Day invasion of fortress Europe was an experience Troy never forgot. His company was part of a regiment that landed with the first wave on Omaha Beach, Normandy. It was a hard fight getting ashore. Once that was accomplished, a more costly battle began with every hedgerow that surrounded farmer's fields near the flat coastal plain. The Germans defended the fields with strategically located machine guns and mortar emplacements. Casualties rose dramatically as the Americans began their breakout from the beachhead. Four days after the invasion, his company was bogged down in the hedgerows when he received his first letter from Gail. Twenty-five years later, he could still recite it word for word.

Somewhere on the English Channel

Dear Troy;

A few words tonight to tell you that I pray every day for your safety and well-being. The invasion is on and I'm overwhelmed by the immensity of the operation. Our ship is now passing large ocean-going tugs pushing sections of portable harbors for unloading the transports. I'm proud to be a part of the effort to free Europe. The task ahead is going to be monstrously wasteful of young lives and I'm frightened by that aspect of this great enterprise.

The Army battalions we are assigned to will release the attached Navy element as soon as our ship drops anchor off the Normandy coast. The courage and dedication of the Army medical units is an inspiration. You men in the front lines are well served by those who will care for your wounds.

I've been thinking a lot about the times we spent together. Occasionally I feel guilty because happiness and warfare are a contradiction and personal feelings seem trivial and selfish in the presence of so much misery and suffering. When I was with you it was easy to forget about the war and the pain associated with it. Thank you for that, my gentle Troy.

I like the idea of setting a rendezvous, even the name incites some excitement and intrigue. I pray that it will be fulfilled. I must close now. Remember that I am with you in spirit. May my love and prayers be your shield of armor and keep you safe.

All my love,

Gail

Troy's company was heavily involved in the slugfest of the hedgerows and was one of the first units to make a breakout to the interior of France. His company had been in the line continuously for weeks. Everyone was numb from fatigue. Finally, his company was ordered to halt and maintain a defensive posture. He and his men breathed easier when fresh troops started to pass through their lines to press the attack forward. Troy's first objective was to insure that his men were getting the hot food he had been promised. They would be out of the line for a day or two.

Troy also sought permission to return to the coast for a few hours to check on Gail. He had received two letters from her since they had left England, and was worried about her safety. He hitched a ride with an artillery spotter plane that landed on the Normandy beach. Troy jumped out of the small aircraft and rushed to Corps headquarters to look up the location of the battalion Gail was assigned to.

A young second lieutenant checked through his roster of units in a file against the wall. He turned to look at Troy.

"Is anything wrong, Lieutenant?" Troy asked, alarmed at his expression.

"Captain, our records show that the surgical unit Ensign Gail Malone was assigned to was destroyed by German artillery fire a week ago. The only survivors were two doctors and an Army medic. I'm sorry…"

Chapter Three

"Are you sure?" Troy had cried.

"You can see for yourself, Captain," answered the lieutenant, placing the folder so that he could examine it. The Army casualty forms were in order. Troy was intimately familiar with them. He felt light-headed and grasped the corner of the desk for support. "Are you all right, Captain?"

Death was not a stranger to him. He had lived with it for two and a half years, and had filled out hundreds of the forms like the one he held in his hand. Gail had been on the roster list and was not among the survivors. He was numb with shock and pain. The futility of it filled him with hate. She was a nurse, a healer of broken bodies. How was it fair that she too be killed along with the combatants? He didn't know what he was going to do. Troy left Corps Headquarters and walked aimlessly down a road filled with heavily loaded tanks, haft-tracks, and trucks on their way to the front. A Jeep slightly grazed Troy rolling him into a nearby ditch. He was unhurt and continued on his way hitching a ride in the Jeep back to his company. The memories were still vivid.

* * *

Now, Troy was sitting in a wheelchair on the deck of the ship as it rounded the point of land known as Diamond Head on the island of Oahu, Hawaii. He had seen it a number of times throughout his military career and was glad to be back in American territory. His body wounds were healing without complications, but the injured leg was still an unknown. It hurt when he tried to move his toes. He was stubborn in his belief that if he moved them enough it would contribute to the circulation of blood and maintain an element of muscle tone.

Nurses, doctors, and therapists descended on the ship as soon as it landed to evaluate each patient and route them to the proper facility for care and treatment. Troy was one of the first to be moved from the ship. He was taken by Army ambulance to Schofield Barracks Hospital located on a mountainous section of land above the Pearl Harbor anchorage.

"Colonel Hansen," announced a young Army Major at the Hospital. "We've just completed a thorough physical on you and I want to discuss your condition. Congratulations on the Distinguished Service Cross."

"Thank you, Major. I don't deserve it as much as the men in my regiment, so I'll wear it in honor of them."

"Well put, Sir. Your torso wounds are exceeding our expectations. X-ray and EKG indicate that they are healing satisfactorily and your vitals are holding normal."

"The Hansens are quick healers," Troy grinned. "What about my leg? Is it going to force me to retire?"

"It would be unfair for me to speculate. We don't know the extent of damage to the nerves or muscles until we remove the cast. I wanted to talk to you about that. X-rays reveal that the tibia has not completely healed. Normally a cast would remain in place. However, I want your permission to remove the cast so that our team of surgeons can evaluate if added surgery needs to be done."

"Of course, I don't mind. I rely on your expertise, Major."

"Prematurely removing of the cast carries an element of risk if you're not careful. A sudden bump or fall could sever that part of the tibia again that has already begun to heal. The surgeons will be able to increase blood circulation and maintain better muscular integrity where they're still intact. We'll design a special brace to partially protect the leg. It won't be as effective as a cast, but it will speed your recovery. Then we'll be able to wrap the leg in this new material that massages your leg muscles while you move about. What do you think, Colonel?"

"Your description sounds logical to me. I approve of anything that will get me back on my feet as soon as possible. I was stationed at Schofield Barracks back in 1950 when the Korean War broke out."

"It hasn't changed much, welcome back, Colonel."

That evening Troy woke in the Army hospital ward. His bed was next to a window with a view of the Pearl Harbor anchorage below. A lonely feeling came over him. He was back on American soil! It should have been a time for celebration and rejoicing. Instead, it brought back the desolate feelings he had been suppressing for years. He had no regrets, but life with his wife, Beth, had not achieved the heights of euphoria he had hoped for. She had never supported his desire to be a career officer in the Army. She disliked the frequent moves required of them, and the uncertainty of what he would be doing. They had loved each other once, but the marital bonds were now stretched to the breaking point.

They stayed together for the sake of their two daughters, Cera, 21 years old, and a student at the University of New Hampshire and Karen, 22 years old, married to an engineer and living in California. Cera was studying to be a journalist. She was inspired to help cure the ills of the world and took on the challenge with youthful idealism. Karen was of a much mellower disposition similar to her Mother. She had cut her college years short in order to become a homemaker. Troy had missed out on some of their childhood activities because he was frequently absent. He was always aware of that fact, and was determined to make up for his absence by creating special memories out of the times they were together. Karen resented the lost time and became closer to her mother in the process. She was a very mature and serious child, older than her years. When she was a teenager the relationship between mother and Karen was more that of friends rather than mother and daughter.

Beth was a good mother to the girls. She always harbored dreams of doing something different rather than spending her days caring for the girls and maintaining a household with a husband that was away for months at a time. She wanted more out of life and let him know that she was going to reach for her own dreams when the children no longer needed her. Troy and Beth did not dislike each other. It was simply a matter of no longer caring. Living together had become a habit, and a routine that was not uncomfortable, yet it fueled Beth's desire for greener pastures. Indifference had become a way of life for some time.

Karen and her husband, Ken Holman, lived in San Francisco. Beth lived with them while Troy had gone off to combat in Vietnam. Troy was anxious to let them know that he was in Hawaii doing okay. Beth answered the phone.

"Hello."

"Is that you, Beth?" asked Troy.

"Yes, Troy. Where are you?" she asked relieved to hear his voice.

"I'm at Schofield Barracks Hospital."

"You've had us worried sick, Troy. The Army called to tell me that you had been wounded and were on a ship that had left Vietnam. Tell me the truth, how are you doing?"

"I've been shot up a little. I'm doing fine except for my leg. I'll probably have a permanent disability. They aren't sure just now. How are the girls and you doing? It's nice to hear your voice again."

"Cera is still at school in Durham. I swear that child has more energy than the two of us combined. Karen and Ken are busy fixing up their house. Ken has a good steady job at an airplane factory. They're happy."

"If you have a pencil and paper handy I'll give you my address and phone number. I'm in a ward instead of a private room. I prefer it this way."

"Aside from the wounds," Beth stated seriously. "I'm sure that things haven't changed between the two of us, but I never wanted to do anything that would hurt you. I've been worried about you."

"I'm okay. I'm sorry that my choice of career pulled us a part. I'm to blame for stubbornly remaining in the Army."

"I've always been proud of you, Troy."

"Where do we go from here, Beth?"

"This is probably not the time to discuss that."

"To the contrary, Beth. I'd say that the family has come to a time and place where everybody has the opportunity to take the road of their choice. I know that you have not been happy for a long time. Whatever it is that you're looking for, I'll never stand in your way. I wish you success and fulfillment."

"All of our friends think I'm crazy. Would it be possible to consider a half way measure, like a separation, for a while?" Beth asked hesitantly.

Troy had expected her request. "I'm sorry, Beth. If you feel that you must follow your dreams, I'm not going to wait around for you to make up your mind. Things have got to change for us."

"Are you saying that you want the separation?" she asked.

"No, I'm not, but I don't want to maintain the status quo either. It's decision-time and I love you enough to want what is best for you. Only you know what that is," Troy answered truthfully.

"Thank you, Troy," she said with a sigh. "We haven't talked together for over a year and we end up having this kind of a conversation. It's monstrous isn't it?"

"My sentiments too, Beth. I've got to go now. It was nice talking with you. I needed to hear a familiar voice."

"I don't hate you, Troy. I hate myself for doing this to you."

"There's plenty of blame to go around. Give Karen a hug from dad and say 'hi' to Cera."

"I will and take care of yourself, Troy."

"Good-bye, Beth."

Troy hung up the phone with trembling hands. Nothing was new. He didn't expect a miracle, but it would have been a welcome discovery if love, as they once knew it, could have returned to welcome him home. His nerves were tattered shreds. He silently wept for hours in the darkness. There was no passion behind the homecoming welcome. He felt insignificant with no place that he could call home. Where did he go from here?

He reviewed his marriage to Beth. The future did not look promising. He recalled an old proverb he had read somewhere: "those who dwell in the past are in danger of losing the future." Unwilling to think of the future, Troy returned again to the more pleasant days of the past and asked himself this question: Were the dreams and visions he and Gail had nurtured together responsible for the failure of his marriage?

* * *

The first time he met Beth she was a Red Cross worker at an Army base in occupied Germany immediately after the war. His father had died suddenly and he was having trouble getting an emergency leave, so he turned to see if the Red Cross could help him expedite the process. Beth was able to arrange it within a few hours. It had been immediately after Germany surrendered and the country was in turmoil. He had flown home on a Military Air Transport plane just in time to attend his father's funeral. Most of the younger men in the small town were still in the service. His mother was not doing very well. Troy was able to convince her, that for the time being, a temporary move into the home of one of her sisters in the small Town of Monson would be the best thing for her. The family homestead was in need of a lot of repairs and Troy contracted with a neighbor to lay a new roof and do other repairs in anticipation of his mother's return.

When Troy returned to Germany, he made a point of stopping by the Red Cross office to thank Beth for her help. She was a vivacious brunette with a carefree attitude and a ready smile. Beth was tall and slender with fine facial features and alert dark brown eyes. She was fun to be with. Most of the time she was positive and up-beat, yet if the occasion required it, she could be serious and reflective. He had always liked that about her because he had a tendency to be overly serious. Together they seemed to make an enjoyable compromise and their friendship grew steadily.

Beth's family was in California. When the war ended in August of 1945, Troy was assigned to a tour of duty at Fort Stewart, Georgia. A month furlough preceded the new duty station. The first thing he did was call Beth who had returned to California prior to his leaving Germany. He flew to San Francisco where he met her parents. They were anxious for their daughter to settle down. All of his leave time was spent with Beth on the west coast. They ended up getting engaged. Ten months later, July 1946, they were married. Karen was born May, 1947 and Cera was born September 1948.

Frequent moves in the Army were a fact of life, so they had purchased a seasonal cottage to serve as a retreat for furloughs, holidays, vacations, etc. in the mountainous regions of northern California. It was a great place to get away from on-base housing which left a lot to be desired. The fact that it was close to Beth's parents also pleased her.

Troy didn't object to California, but the lure of the Maine woods was strong within him. Given the opportunity, he would have preferred being somewhere in New England than on the west coast. It was a basic difference that never got resolved and he did not press the issue. Beth would have balked at leaving California.

The morning after Troy called Beth his phone rang while he was eating breakfast.

"Hello."

"Hi, Dad," cried an excited voice he was happy to hear. "I just talked to mom and Karen. She gave me your number."

"It's so nice to hear your voice, sweetheart. I've missed you a lot," Troy exclaimed, happy to hear from his younger daughter.

"We were worried out of our minds over the news that you were wounded. Without covering anything up, how are you doing?" It was a plea from Cera who liked straight talk.

"I'm fine, except for my right leg. I still have it but I'm afraid it will leave me limited. How much I don't know yet. That's the truth, young lady."

"How long are you going to be there, Daddy?"

"I'm not sure, a month maybe," answered Troy. He felt better already after hearing her voice. Her energy and love of life was contagious. She was fun to be with.

"That settles it. I'm coming to Hawaii to be with you for a while. I just finished school. Mom wanted me to come out to the cottage with her but I can't do that knowing that you're lying wounded in a hospital."

"That sounds great to me, Cera. There isn't anything in the world I'd rather do than give my baby girl a hug."

"Okay, Daddy, I'll be there as soon as I can make travel arrangements. I've got lots of things to talk to you about. You

24

didn't tell mother about your Distinguished Service Cross did you?"

"How did you know about that?"

"Why didn't you say anything to mom? I'm so proud of you. If you must know, I learned about the medal from an ROTC Lieutenant at school. I dated him a couple of times and asked him to look into your status. I was worried about the seriousness of your wounds."

"Starting your investigative techniques a little early aren't you young lady?" he laughed. It was typical of her.

"I just couldn't sit and not know about you, Dad. I love you very much and will see you soon."

"I love you too, Honey. I'll be waiting for you."

His baby girl was growing up!

Chapter Four

Cera Hansen boarded the TWA plane at Boston's Logan Airport. It was a direct flight to San Francisco where she changed planes for Honolulu. She had laughing brown eyes and a small slightly upturned nose. She wore her auburn hair cut short just below her ears because it was easy to care for. A small amount of lipstick on her lips accented their sensuousness. She moved quickly and decisively. She was short and petite, a lady of many moods. Those who thought they knew her were surprised at the depth of her psyche.

Most people liked her with the exception of those who were prone to put on airs of superiority, or were impressed with their own self-importance. Whenever she encountered that type, Cera took delight in puncturing their inflated ego. She liked straight talk and eagerly dismissed phonies. Quick and intelligent, she was a happy person and generated a large circle of friends. That trait came from her mother. The serious side of her came from her father to whom she was devoted.

She took her seat on the large aircraft and watched Boston Harbor disappear as they took off over the Atlantic Ocean. Cera leaned back in her seat and thought about her father. She was aware of her mother's wishes and it angered her to think that she could be so callous in her feelings. Her dad was coming home, a hero from the third war of his Army career, in need of all of the love and support the family could embellish on him. They owed him more than their mother seemed willing to give.

As Cera grew older and wiser, she realized that he was typical of many of the combat veterans. Most suffered from deep and lasting psychic wounds. As a group they were taciturn, impatient, and uneasy when asked about their wartime experiences. Silence was the norm. If a person was trying to impress the world that he was a combat veteran by telling stories of his experiences, there was a good chance that person was not what he claimed to be. Most veterans remained mute for most of their lives!

When Cera was a little girl she could "feel" the horrors that her daddy kept to himself. Sometimes he would sit and stare at the horizon as if he was looking for something or someone. She always saw that dark shadow of sadness in the hollow recess of his eyes. He never said anything, but the torment was obvious to those who cared for him. Karen and her mother never looked deep enough to share his pain the way Cera was able to do.

She was only four years old when he came home from the Korean War. He was a man at the edge of his emotional resources. She sensed the magnitude and the depth of the pain he never complained about. Cera was drawn to him more than ever in that dark period. He was a gentle, loving father. She was always searching for some way to make the haunting look of despair disappear and never come back. Outwardly he never favored one over the other, but he and Cera were in tune with each other, both aware of the special bond that existed between them.

Karen and Cera graduated from a small town high school north of San Francisco on the coast. It was their mother's hometown. Troy had returned home from a tour of duty in Germany. He and Beth agreed that the girls should stay in one place for the four years they would be in high school. Cera remembered her senior prom. It was a high point in her senior year. Troy and Beth were voted as honorary chaperones. Cera was so proud of her parents. They were an attractive couple. Her dad was especially handsome in his uniform.

Kurt Jenkins was Cera's date that night. He was a short chunky young man who did well on the football team. Cera was dressed in a pale yellow gown. Kurt was very attentive to her. She was a very popular girl. Several boys had asked her for a date, so when she said yes to Kurt he was the envy of many of his friends. There were two Indian students in their class, a brother and a sister who came to the dance. They belonged to one of the local tribes in northwest California. Several people were upset that the two were present. Their discovery unleashed an unspoken undercurrent of racial bigotry in the auditorium. It was more than Cera could believe, and it bothered her. She was good friends to both of them. When Cera's escort, Kurt, made some offensive remark about them she slapped him across the face and walked off the dance floor without him.

Neither of the Indian students danced. They sat alone bearing the silence and unfriendliness with stoic dignity and grace. Troy and Beth saw the intentional neglect, looked at each other and simultaneously came up with the same solution. Beth wore a yellow dress similar to Cera's. They left their seats of honor beside the orchestra and approached the Indian brother and sister, Ben and Vera.

Troy bowed to Vera and smiled at her. "May I have the privilege of dancing with you, young lady?"

Vera was uncomfortable being the object of neglect until she heard the tall attractive soldier speak to her in a calm respectful way. Her eyes lit up, returning his smile.

"It would be my pleasure, Sir," she said, accepting the arm he offered to her.

Beth did the same thing to Ben. The two couples circled the auditorium several times oblivious to the other dancers. Cera watched them from the sidelines swelled with pride and loving them more than ever. Cera later learned from Vera what her father had said to her: "You're a lovely young lady. Hold your head up high and be proud of what and who you are. Those who try to scorn or belittle you do so because it makes them feel superior, when in reality they have proven themselves to be inferior. Don't give them a chance to make you feel that way. Look them in the eye and let them see the pride and dignity that has always been a part of your people's legacy as the first Americans. You're a very good dancer. I hope I don't step on your toes." Vera had smiled at him when he joked about himself.

When the dance set was over Troy and Beth asked Ben and Vera to come and sit with them near the orchestra. The next set began shortly and Cera approached Ben, asking him to dance with her. He beamed at her request and accepted. Kurt, ashamed at his hasty remarks, saw what Cera was doing. He reciprocated asking Vera to dance with him. To his delight he found that she was light on her feet and an excellent dancer. She made him look better than he really was.

Ben and Vera danced every dance for the rest of the evening. At the end, as everyone was leaving the auditorium, Vera was waiting outside near the entrance door for Troy and Beth. She walked up to them as they started down the steps.

"Mr. And Mrs. Hansen," she announced in a clear melodious voice. "Ben and I want to thank you for your kindness. I'll remember what you told me, Major Hansen. Thank you again and goodnight." She kissed Troy on the cheek and hugged Beth. That had been three years ago, and Cera still kept in touch with them.

Cera took a cab from the airfield to Schofield Barracks, the large Army base in the mountains a few miles from Pearl Harbor. The hospital was filled with wounded soldiers. Some sat on the veranda overlooking the harbor anchorage and Ford Island. Others exercised on the walkways. She had checked her bag at the terminal, uncertain of where she was going to stay, and carried her purse over her left shoulder as she confidently walked to the entrance. Dressed in a light green pant suit and wearing a pair of sunglasses Cera drew a number of whistles from admiring soldiers. She waved her hand in acknowledgment and smiled to the men. "Thank you guys – love you all too," she cried out to them.

One of the wounded soldiers held the door open for her. "Welcome to the hospital, Ma'am."

"Thank you. I'm here to see my dad. I wish you well."

The duty desk was manned by an Army captain wearing a name tag. "What can I do for you, Miss?"

"I've come to see my father, Colonel Troy Hansen."

"You'll find him in a wheelchair on the balcony, Miss Hansen. Go down the hallway and take your first left. He's been a wonderful patient. You'll be good for him."

"Thank you, Captain."

Cera found her way to the balcony recognizing her father sitting near the railing watching the ships in the harbor below. She caught her breath, he looked so old and drawn. His hair had turned much whiter than the last time she had seen him. She called out to him.

"Is that you, Daddy?"

Troy turned toward the familiar voice and saw her running towards him. He choked up reaching for her. She kneeled down to embrace him.

"My darling little girl, I'm so glad to see you. You'll never know how much I've missed you, Honey."

"I do know, Dad. I've been so worried about you." She noted the look in his eyes. The horrors he must have seen to look that way brought tears to her eyes.

"You look wonderful, Cera. Just a few minutes ago I heard some of the men whistling. Was that for you?" he asked, smiling. Tears of joy could not be denied.

"Yes, they were great."

"You must be used to that kind of attention by now. Young soldiers do have an eye for pretty girls."

"Flattery will get you anything," she teased him. "Now tell me truthfully. How are you doing? I can see that you need rest and a diet that will put a little more weight on your bones. What about your injuries?"

"The doctors are surprised at my recovery from surgery of the bullets wounds in my upper torso. I've lost a spleen but a person can get along without one. The bullet that penetrated a small portion of my lungs still gives me shortness of breath, but it's lessening every day. My leg is still an unknown, Cera. At least I still have it and am thankful for that."

"I'm thankful that you're here safe. Hopefully, your leg will terminate your commission," exclaimed Cera emphatically.

"Cera, what are saying?"

"It's true, Dad. You've seen enough soldiering for a lifetime. It's time for a new generation to take over. I don't want to see you in combat again and I'm sure I speak for Mom and Karen."

"My you look good to me, Honey. I was afraid you'd already be committed to a job or something. I've spoken to your Mother…"

A nurse interrupted them. "Do you need anything, Colonel?"

"Not at the moment nurse. This is my daughter, Cera. She just flew in from New Hampshire to see me."

"You've come a long ways, Miss Hansen. It'll soon be supper time for the patients. May I order a tray for you to eat with your Dad?"

"That would be nice, nurse, thank you. I'm not fussy so I'll have what Dad is having."

"I'll see to it. The two of you can eat out here or would you prefer a little more privacy in one of the empty rooms?"

"This will be fine, nurse," answered Troy. "No special privileges, please."

"I can't think of a nicer place to dine with my Dad than right here on the balcony. The view is spectacular," Cera exclaimed.

"Have you been keeping in touch with your mother regularly?"

"I call or write her more than she does me," said Cera, raising her hands in exasperation. "I don't know what she's thinking, Dad. Karen says that she doesn't see that much of her either."

"Your mother has been an unhappy person for a long time. The life of a soldier's wife is not an easy one. I understand that. She's reached a point in her life when she wants more than she has had over the years. It's that simple and that complex."

"You're right, but others have the gumption to stick it out," declared Cera, not accepting her father's defense of her mother. "She has always liked the prestige of being an officer's wife. The long absences have made her unsure of herself. If I didn't know better, I'd swear that she was having an affair with another man."

"Cera," cried Troy stunned by her directness. "Don't be that harsh unless you've got evidence to substantiate it... Can you?"

"No, I haven't any way of proving it," she responded honestly. "I don't understand her. She's come this far in her marriage. Now that Karen and I are adults pursuing our own lives and you are about to retire from the Army, the best times of your lives can be ahead of you two. It should be a time when you can share things without family obligations and burdensome bills getting in the way."

"I was kind of hoping of something along those lines. If we had a chance to be together maybe we could make up for lost opportunities." Troy made room on his chair tray for the orderly bringing supper. "The food here is not bad, Cera. You must be hungry. The peanuts and crackers they feed you on the planes are not very filling."

"I am hungry," answered Cera. An orderly placed a tray on the bench beside her. "Thank you very much. It looks good."

"Is there anything else I can get either of you?" the orderly asked.

"I'm all set, young man. Thank you."

"So am I, orderly."

Troy watched Cera. At times she was still like a little girl. Small things pleased her, and her enthusiasm was reflected in her expressive eyes. There was an aura of expectation and wholesomeness that drew people to her. He was more proud of Cera and Karen than anything else in his life. They had made it complete and worthwhile. Cera still had some of the same mannerisms she had as a small child like sticking her little finger straight out when she picked up a fork or a pencil or a cup of coffee. Boys were attracted to her like flies to honey. She dated occasionally and had legions of friends because she was a good friend.

They ate in silence. It was comforting to Troy just to have her near. In the short time she had been with her father, she saw a difference in him. His eyes were brighter and he seemed to be more energized. It showed in his body language and the way he spoke. Left by himself he tolerated the days and simply let them slip by. Each one had been the same. Cera's presence had changed that. Troy felt the fight coming back to him, and the desire to get well was stronger than ever. The future had promise even if Beth was not going to be a part of it. It was not an ending, but a beginning. Before Cera came, he had given up without realizing it.

Hearing Cera talk the way she did about her mother filled him with a resolve he had been debating within himself. It would have been natural for him to go to California when his leg was well enough to be discharged. He had never liked California and yearned for the Maine woods. He made up his mind that that is where he was going. He wanted to be near his own kind of people. Most of his adult life Troy had followed orders and done what had to be done for his country and his family. If he was medically discharged from the Army he had made up his mind to listen to his inner yearnings. Arriving at that decision was comforting. He was optimistic about future prospects. His spirits soared as soon as he had established specific goals for himself.

"How are you and Karen going to feel if your mother and I get a divorce?"

"Have you two arrived at that point?" Cera questioned.

"No, but she asked if we could separate for a while so that she could try it out so to speak. I refused. If we did that and she wanted a reconciliation I'd always feel used and second best. I don't want any part of such an arrangement."

"Karen and I love both of you and I don't think we have the wisdom to advise you, Daddy. You've had over twenty-four years together. It's a shame that you can't recapture what it was that brought you together in the first place."

"I know it'll be hard on you girls and I would not want to put either of you in the position of choosing one over the other. That wouldn't be fair."

"You talk as if it's a done deal, Dad," exclaimed Cera uncomfortable talking about the subject. "Did you and mom have words when she spoke to you?"

"Yes and no," replied Troy wondering if he was premature in bringing Cera into the conversation. "I don't want things to continue the way they have been. I want more than that. She wants to stay in California. I have a strong desire to get to Maine. I want to feel snug and at ease in a warm home when the north winds blow and howl through the trees. I want to be able to drop a fish line in a stream or a pond to catch trout and salmon. I've dreamed of returning to Maine for so long I can almost taste it. I've been away too long. I need that to be whole again. I'm not sure you can understand my concept of home and how strongly I feel about it."

Cera watched her father defend his position. He spoke with passion and his eyes lit up whenever he mentioned Maine. She got up from her seat and hugged him.

"I love you, Daddy. None of us, including mother, have ever completely appreciated what you've been through in three wars. If your heart tells you to go to Maine, then follow it with my blessings. Return to your roots. If Mother doesn't want to go along with you, then that's her choice. Over the years we've been selfish, always thinking what was good for the family. At this stage of your life, you deserve a chance to choose what is best for you without any justification."

"I'm lucky to have a girl like you, Cera. I appreciate your support. How were things in New Hampshire? Who was this ROTC instructor you dated?"

"Durham never changes. Lieutenant Collins is studying for a master's degree in engineering. We've dated a few times. Nothing serious, we're simply good friends."

"He sounds like a go-getter."

Cera had been thinking about her father's return to Maine. "If you were to go to Maine, where would you go? The old family home has been sold for quite a while since grandmother passed away."

"I haven't progressed that far yet, Honey. I plan to propose a move to your mother as an alternative for us. We could purchase a small place near a stream or a lake."

"Ah, I have some information you'll want to hear," Cera announced triumphantly.

"What have you got?"

"This spring I went up to Lily Bay on Moosehead Lake with some students for a camping trip. While we were there I drove to Kokadjo to visit Mr. and Mrs. Cooper. Did you know that Mr. Cooper died this past winter?"

"No, I had no way of knowing," Troy answered, saddened to hear of the death of his old Army buddy. One of the finest officers it was his privilege to serve with. Troy had been a battalion Executive Officer in Colonel Dale Cooper's regiment in Korea. "I'm sorry to hear that. How's Mrs. Cooper handling things?"

34

"She was still devastated when I saw her. What a lovely gracious person she is. I remember we went to their place several times while we were growing up. It was an exciting place to visit."

"Yes, it was. I'm glad you went to see her. They were a wonderful pair, devoted to each other. I must stop by to see her when I go back. It's sad to lose such good people. This country was well served by Dale Cooper. He fought valiantly in three wars and lost their daughter in World War Two."

"Mrs. Cooper mentioned her to me. When I left she hugged me and said that I reminded her of their daughter, Heather. She cried when she said Heather's name," recalled Cera. "My heart went out to her."

"Was that what you wanted to tell me, Cera?" asked Troy.

"Mrs. Cooper told me that she was considering selling the cabin and lease they have with the Great Northern Paper Company. She thought of returning to her native village to work in an infirmary as long as she's physically able to make a contribution to her people's welfare."

"Bless her heart," added Troy, thinking about the things Cera told him. "If she wants to sell that place, I'd buy it in a heartbeat!"

Chapter Five

"You would, Daddy?"

"Sure, if the price is within our pay scale. It's a beautiful place. Dale and Ashley were very happy there. He originally came from Monson."

"I thought you'd react this way, so I briefly mentioned it to Mrs. Cooper. She said that you could have first refusal on it. They had no family to leave it to. I can tell you that it was not an easy decision for her to make. The winter months there are severe and difficult to handle alone."

"I would imagine," Troy replied, looking at Cera. "What do you think about it?"

"I mentioned it to you as something to think about. If you end up purchasing it I'd like to stay there with you."

"Will you wait on me and do all of the work in the cabin?" Troy teased.

"We'd have to discuss it," laughed Cera. "Seriously though, Dad, what would you do if you purchased it? I know you would never be one to sit on the porch and vegetate in a rocking chair."

"I've been approached by a couple of news service people that were in Vietnam about the prospect of doing occasional background pieces on military related subjects and how they may affect governmental policies. I was flattered by the offer. The more I thought about it the more excited I became. I could do as much or as little as I want."

"Wow, that sounds great. Can I influence your very conservative outlook with a small dose of selective liberalism here and there in your essays?" Cera asked impishly.

"I'll listen to what you have to say, but that may be as far as it goes," Troy laughed. He hadn't laughed in a long time. Cera was good for him.

"I'm glad for you, Daddy."

They reminisced about old times until it was dark and the air on the balcony was getting damp. Cera spoke to her father about a place to sleep, and he told her that arrangements were made for her to stay at the Schofield Barracks hospitality center for as long as she was visiting him. She said goodnight to him when the orderlies came to wheel him back into the ward. Cera took a cab to retrieve her bags in Pearl City and returned to the hospitality center. Her room was Spartan, but clean and secure, typical of an Army installation.

* * *

That night, Troy slept better than he had in a long time. Before he dozed off to sleep he recalled his last visit to Dale and Ashley Cooper's isolated log cabin north of Moosehead Lake. The cabin was located on a series of cliffs several feet above the small Lake of Three Sorrows. It was named in honor of an Indian mother who had been picking berries with her two small children, a boy and a girl. They were crossing the lake when their canoe became overturned in a sudden squall, which was not uncommon in the early fall months. All three were drowned. Dale had told him that sometimes when the moon was full and the lake was like shining glass, he and Ashley have heard the sounds of a woman softly crying. They came from the western side of the lake where the canoe was swamped.

Dale Cooper was a tall man with a medium build and an easy-going temperament. He was a gentleman from the old school and a superb combat leader. He was fearless in battle and compassionate in the care of his men. His calm demeanor masked an iron resolve to carry out any mission assigned him. Troy would have followed him to hell and back if asked to do so. The men he led not only respected him, they genuinely liked the man for his unpretentious ways.

Over the years, visits to the log cabin were a memorable experience for anyone fortunate enough to make the trip. The last time Troy saw Dale and Ashley together was the summer of 1960. The entire Hansen family stayed for several days. They had fun swimming, canoeing, and playing baseball on a flat portion of the rocky formations. The Maine woods have a well-earned reputation of generating healthy appetites. They ate vast amounts of food. Dale in particular recalled the large trout and fresh water salmon they cooked over an open grill in front of the cabin. There was something powerfully calming about the place. Everyone that had ever been there said the same thing. The Coopers were noted for their graciousness as hosts, and for the harmonious atmosphere that always prevailed in their home.

Dale, a professional forester, was Woodlands Manager for the Great Northern Paper Company. One day Troy accompanied Dale to a forest harvesting operation north of the impressive Ripogenus Dam, which controlled the flow of water and pulpwood from remote regions of the State to the paper mills at Millinocket. They owned thousands of acres of forest land in central and northern Maine.

Dale had confided to him that his love of the land and his job as a forester were responsible for maintaining his sanity during a painful thirteen year period when he was rejected by Ashley. Ultimately they were reunited and their life was filled with a new dimension of happiness. Their home reflected the harmony and contentment that existed between them. It was their reward for years of separation and the faithfulness they carried in their hearts. Troy felt privileged to be their friend.

In April 1965 Ashley had written to Beth that Dale had passed away. Beth had failed to notify Troy. Death occurred while he was fishing off the dock at their home on the Lake of Three Sorrows. The end was as gentle and quick as death can be. Ashley saw him lying on the dock and rushed to him. She checked for a pulse, but he had already gone, and her world collapsed. They had a wide circle of friends which helped her accept his death, but it did not relieve the anguish of losing a true soul mate.

When Cera started school at the University Of New Hampshire, she made a point of visiting Ashley at least once a year when she could break away from her studies. There was a special bond between the slender white-haired Canadian Cree

Indian lady and the young energetic Cera. Occasionally, Ashley drove to Durham to visit Cera and take her out to a seaside restaurant on the coast. Ashley was fond of fried clams. She was a beautiful woman, warm and sincere without a trace of pretense. Cera was always proud to introduce Ashley to her friends at school. She confided to Cera that those visits helped sustain her during the loneliest time of her life.

During one of Ashley's visits to Durham, Cera learned that her native Cree name was Iowaka. She still had family ties to the native village at the northern end of Lac Saint Jean and owned a cabin that her mother had lived in before she died years ago. She confided to Cera that she was contemplating a return to the village where she could work in the area infirmary as a nurse. She still maintained her nurse's certification in Canada as well as the United States. By spending her remaining time in the service of her people she would be fulfilling an old dream, and giving thanks for the rewarding life she was able to live. She was certain that it would meet with Dale's approval. It was an act in tribute to her dead daughter, Heather, who was killed in action in World War Two. She had gone to the same Nursing School as Ashley and had volunteered in the Army Nurse Corps when the war began.

The medical team at the Schofield Barracks Hospital focused their attention and expertise on Troy's leg. The first thing they did was remove the cast. He was conscious all the time. They probed and examined his infected leg thoroughly and took more x-rays, which indicated that his main leg bone, the tibia, had been broken in three places. Added surgery was necessary to insert stainless steel pins to hold the fragmented bones firmly in place. In time, they would be capable of supporting his leg and allow him to walk and run. The prognosis was that he would have a permanent limp and would need corrective shoes for that leg. It also meant that his Army career was coming to an end. As soon as the leg began to heal and no further complications were involved he could be sent to the mainland, possibly within a week.

Later that evening, after the surgery was completed, Cera was sitting beside his bed in the recovery room. She watched him as he started to come out from under the influence of the anesthesia. He had trouble focusing his eyes and failed to recognize Cera. A nurse entered the room to announce that Troy was going to be out for the rest of the night with little chance of waking.

Cera thanked the nurse and returned to her room at the hospitality center where she made a call to her mother and Karen in California.

"Hello, Mom?"

"Cera, it's nice to hear from you. Are you in Pearl Harbor with your father?" her Mother asked.

"Yes, Mom. I'm calling to let you know that Dad's spirits are high. His leg was operated on today. Without going into detail, he'll end up with some deformity to his leg and will walk with a limp of some kind and need a corrective shoe for that foot."

"Oh my. Is that going to force him to retire from the Army?"

"I think so. Time will tell. I've talked to him about that and I think he's ready to retire anyway."

"I had that feeling the last time we spoke," Beth told her.

"What are your thoughts, Mother? Where do you and Dad go from here?" Cera knew the question would not be appreciated, but she had to know what was ahead for her father.

"You don't beat around the bush do you, Cera?" Beth asked defiantly.

"Dad deserves to know how things stand and I'd like to know also. The two of you have much to look forward to in the immediate future. Dad's wounds could have been worse. We have much to be thankful for."

"I know Cera, I'm glad that he's recovering so well..."

"You're not answering my question, Mom."

"I don't want to answer when you cross examine me that way."

"I'm sorry. I was only thinking of Dad's future. He's on the edge Mom, or haven't you given that any thought?"

"Don't forget who you're talking to, young lady. For your information, I've thought a lot about his welfare. If you insist on prying," said Beth in an exasperated tone. "I believe that it's for the best that we go our separate paths while there's still time for each of us to follow our dreams. That's not the same as saying that I hate your father. To the contrary I respect and admire him for the fine qualities that have made him the good soldier he is. I can't tell you why my urge to want something different is so strong, but it's beckoning me to make the move. I don't do it without regrets or the thought that it's an outrageous act, maybe a mid-life crisis. Your father has already told me that if I take that route there's no turning back. I find it frightening and liberating at the same time. Can you understand what I'm trying to say, Cera?"

"Yes I can, Mom. I don't like it but I can understand your desire to fly higher and further than you have while the family needed you. I'm not judging you, Mother, I'm simply saddened that things have deteriorated to this point. He needs all of us more than ever right now."

"I'm glad that you're not judging me. I don't want to abandon your father at a time when he needs our support the most. I honestly think that, deep inside, he's known that we were not meant to travel the distance together."

"I'm not sure what he thinks. We better close, this call will cost a fortune. I'm staying with Dad until he goes back to the mainland at least, maybe longer. I'll keep in touch with you and Karen to give you an update on his progress. How's my big sister doing?"

"You'll be pleased to know that she's pregnant."

"Wow, Karen pregnant," exclaimed Cera excitedly. "That's wonderful. I'll soon be an aunt imagine that! Give her a hug for me and tell her we love her. Dad will be excited about the news too."

"I'll tell her. Give our best to your father. Tell him that I continue to pray for him. I love you, Cera."

"I love you too, Mom."

Troy was still sound asleep when she showed up at the hospital the next morning. He had been moved back into the ward with six other patients. Troy had insisted on being treated the same as an enlisted soldier, refusing a private room, which is what his rank merited.

In the far corner of the ward was a young soldier not much older than Cera. He sat motionless in his bed and stared out the window looking at the mountain ranges in the distance. Cera had introduced herself to most of the men in the ward. Her outgoing disposition was welcome by most of the patients. A couple had asked her to play cards. She accepted the offer and spent some time with them, recognizing how lonely they were far from home. Breakfast trays had been cleared away. Most of the men talked with their buddies, listened to their radios, anything that helped to fill up the day. The long hours of idleness was as difficult to bear as their injuries.

Cera's presence in the ward was a topic of discussion. Some thought that since she was the daughter of a full colonel she would not want to bother with the enlisted patients. They were wrong. She circulated freely among the men, offering to help in any way that she could. By the end of her first day she learned most of their names and home towns. Home was the main topic of discussion. The sergeant closest to Troy's bed was still confined to his bed with two legs in traction. Unable to move about, he maintained a running commentary on current events with his neighbor. He held his hand up to get Cera's attention. She approached his bed with a smile.

"What can I do for you, Sergeant Hastings?" she asked in a low voice.

"Do you see that guy at the end of the room?"

"Yes, I haven't met him yet. He's been silent since I came to visit my father."

"He's a quiet one. We just learned that we have a celebrity in our midst. His name is Warrant Officer John Lamprey. He was a helicopter pilot that disobeyed orders to retrieve several wounded soldiers on the battlefield. He made four trips back to the fire-fight. On his last pickup, he was hurt pretty bad by enemy ground gunnery, but he managed to bring the helicopter back to friendly lines. He's just been nominated to receive the Medal of Honor."

"That's our nation's highest decoration for courage under fire. You have a right to be proud of him. How badly is he hurt?" asked Cera. She knew that the soldier was aware of her, yet, every time she looked in his direction he turned his head away.

"He lost an arm and may lose a leg. His body was full of shrapnel. The badly wounded man in number three bed was one of the men he picked up under heavy enemy fire. Those helo pilots are number one to me. I owe my life to the steady nerves of a pilot like him. We rate the pilots right at the top of our lists along with the Army medics."

"Should I say 'hi' and congratulate him?"

"Sure. Anyone would like a visit from a pretty girl like you," he smiled.

"Sergeant Hastings you have a mischievous gleam in your eye," she said, returning his smile.

"That's what everyone tells me. I'd introduce you to him but as you can see, I'm all hung up," he replied with a wry look on his face.

"You're impossible, Sergeant!" she exclaimed good-naturedly. That attitude and frame of mind was going to carry the doughty Sergeant Hastings through whatever was ahead of him!

Cera walked over to Lamprey's bed to introduce herself. "Hello, Mister Lamprey. I'm Cera Hansen. I've been visiting my father on the other side of the ward. The sergeant next to him just told me that you've been nominated for the Medal of Honor. I wanted to congratulate you. It's a great honor."

Warrant Officer Lamprey had close-cropped dark hair and a fair complexion. His deep-set eyes had a haunting look about them. He didn't look at you, he looked through you. It was unnerving. His left sleeve hung empty on the white sheets. Several tubes were attached to his body from bottles hanging on a rack above his head. It was difficult for Cera to determine, but she expected that he would be tall and slim. He had delicate facial features.

"Thank you, Miss Hansen," he said in a strained voice.

"Is there anything I can get for you? There's a real good PX near the hospital. I could run there if you need anything. My father is resting from surgery. I'd rather be useful than just hang around waiting for him to recover."

"I'm not in the mood for anything. Thanks for asking though," Lamprey replied with an anxious look on his face.

"Where are you from?" she asked. Her experience around Army bases most of her life indicated that the quickest way to cut the awkwardness of talking with strangers was to ask about their hometown. Most were homesick and, next to their families, most soldiers were ready to talk about where they grew up. It was a place they all related to and yearned to return.

"I'm from Maine. A small town on the coast near Bar Harbor," Lamprey answered turning his head to look at her.

His response was encouraging. "That part of Maine is beautiful. My father is also from Maine. He graduated from the University of Maine at Orono and joined the Army right after graduation. I'm going to the University of New Hampshire."

"What are you studying, Miss Hansen? I went to the University of Maine, too. Your dad and I have that in common."

Two doctors and a nurse stopped by John Lamprey's bedside and began to enclose it with the privacy curtains suspended from the ceiling. Cera excused herself returning to the seat at her father's bed. He was breathing steady. She studied the relaxed look on his face. His arm twitched as if he had a muscle spasm and his mouth opened twice without making a sound. She came closer putting her ear close to his face and listened.

Troy whispered three words: "No, not Gail."

Chapter Six

Troy's facial muscles contracted for several seconds and relaxed. Just as Cera sat down in her chair, a sharp piercing cry filled the ward.

"No, not my leg..."

Cera knew that it was the young helicopter pilot, John Lamprey. The doctors must have brought bad news to him. She sat and contemplated just how she would feel if she had lost an arm and later was told that she was going to lose a leg. A cold chill ran through her body. She had a unique gift of being able to place herself in other people's positions and acknowledge their pain. She felt sorry for the soldier. There was something hauntingly tragic about him that touched her.

"Good morning, Cera," greeted Troy. The loud scream wrenched him awake. The minute he heard it, he knew it was Lamprey. The suffering that took place within veteran's hospitals was rarely described to the American public and few ever made the effort to see for themselves. Every case was exceptional and was begging to be told. Some ended in tragic circumstances. As much bravery and courage was shown within the sterile white walls of the hospital, as was displayed on the battlefield, and it generally remained unheralded.

Cera's visit had fueled an awareness, on her part, of the suffering endured by those few who defended the freedom so often taken for granted. Freedom was not free. She had heard that expression often over the years. Here in the hospital wards she was able to put names and faces to the sacrifices. The price tag was immense and immeasurable. The full magnitude of pain and suffering was born by young soldiers at the threshold of life and by the tears of weeping mothers.

"Good morning, Dad. You were sleeping soundly. How do you feel?" she asked.

"I hate waking up with that numb feeling you have coming out from under the anesthesia," answered Troy impatiently. "I'll bet that cry I heard came from Lamprey."

"Yes. I was sitting with him for a few seconds while you were waking up. The doctors visited him while I was there. A few minutes later he was screaming in protest. Very likely they informed him that his leg had to be amputated. What a horrible piece of news to accept. I don't blame him for screaming."

"He's a quiet patient. I've talked to him, but he doesn't have much to say."

"He was a helicopter pilot. He's been nominated for the Medal Of Honor."

"That's one award I respect without qualification," Troy replied in a serious voice. "I feel lucky about my injuries. My leg feels kind of numb from the operation, but it feels lighter. I should have better mobility with this smaller cast and brace than I had before with the full cast. At least I'll be able to keep it. Poor John, he's just a young kid your age."

"I know, Dad. Did he tell you that he was from Maine too? Someplace near Bar Harbor," said Cera.

"Another Mainiac! The state of Maine has produced some fine warriors over the years. The Maine National Guard unit I went off to war with in World War Two was one of the best I ever served with."

"Dad, I called Mom last night to give her and Karen an update on your progress. I have some good news and some bad news for you," announced Cera.

"I'll take the bad news first. I can guess what it's all about."

"Mom has made up her mind to go her separate way as soon as you're well. Without descriptions of why or how come, it probably is the best thing for the two of you."

"Are you mature enough to be sure of that?" he pointedly asked Cera.

"No, it's just a gut instinct, Dad. If the two of you were to try and hold it together it would eventually come to the same place, leaving both of you exhausted and more bitter. You've given it your best shot. I've asked myself why mom isn't here with you. If my husband was badly injured and in a hospital, I'd be there with him, no matter how difficult it would be."

"I'm sure you would, young lady, and your husband will be a very fortunate person. Where did you gain so much wisdom all of a sudden?" Troy asked proudly. He could never tell her how much it meant to have her with him.

"I'm simply telling you the way it is. You always liked straight talk, Colonel Hansen," Cera replied.

"I know you are, Cera, but there's something inherently sad about breaking up a marriage of several years. I won't deceive you. I've always had the feeling that we'd arrive at this point sooner or later. No matter how you rationalize it, a broken marriage is a failure. A plain and simple defeat. There'll be no rejoicing on my part."

"I didn't mean to depress you, Daddy. Don't take it that way. I have some good news too, so clear your mind of all those negative thoughts."

"What are you trying to say?"

"I'm going to be an aunt and you're going to be a grandfather, Karen's pregnant."

"No kidding?" exclaimed Troy. "That's great news. How far along is she in her pregnancy?"

Another cry of protest erupted from the far corner of the ward. Orderlies and nurses scuffled to place John Lamprey on a mobile stretcher.

"I'm sorry, Son. This has got to be done soon or you're going to die from gangrene," exclaimed a doctor in a soothing tone, giving the young soldier an injection while the orderlies held him. The screams continued for a few seconds and tapered off to muffled groans and then, silence. They quickly wheeled him down the corridor to the operating room.

"The poor kid," Troy shook his head. "Some soldiers just keep on giving of themselves… We must pray for him. He's going to need all the help he can get."

Cera was saddened by the incident. The young helicopter pilot was facing a more formidable foe at this moment in the operating room than he did on the battlefield. She was touched by the depths of the tragedy taking place here and in veteran's hospitals all across the land. Few citizens appreciated, or were aware of, the magnitude of despair and trauma the veterans were subjected to. In that moment of discovery she looked at her father and saw him in a different light. The horror he must have seen and experienced in three wars during his Army career, she could never imagine. He had earned the right to live in peace for the rest of his live.

Two days later, Troy's leg was doing much better. The doctors told him that if he continued without any complications, they could send him to the mainland in a few days. Cera and Troy attended the daily movies shown in the recreation and activity room. One day after his operation, John Lamprey was wheeled into the room beside them in a special electric wheelchair steered by a knob on the right arm rest. His left leg had been amputated slightly above the knee. That fact left him sullen and morose, self-conscious of his limitations, and he rarely spoke or acknowledged anyone around him. He was living in his own private hell.

The evening movies were shown in the ward with a white sheet hung on a wall. They watched the movie *Shane,* with Alan Ladd. It was a favorite of many of the veterans. The sad ending showing the small boy calling after Shane left everyone in a pensive mood. When the lights came on, Cera turned to look at Lamprey. He avoided her glance and turned his chair away from her. She and Troy visited with several of the patients around them. Cera had promised a corporal that she would play a game or two of cribbage, she excused herself to locate a deck of cards and a cribbage board. The game could take hours. Cera was a much appreciated visitor. Several patients sat around the cribbage players and watched. Some bantered with Cera. She had a quiet winsome quality about her and the patients accepted her as part of their family. She tried to make them feel good about themselves but they ended up making her feel even better. Their unquenchable spirit and hope for the future was a joy to experience.

Troy started to wheel himself back to the ward and noticed that Lamprey was lying flat on his bed staring at the ceiling. Troy casually rolled to his bedside.

"Hello, Warrant Officer," greeted Troy, stopping where Lamprey could see him. "My daughter tells me that we're the only two men in the hospital from Maine. That makes us a distinct minority. I want to congratulate you on being nominated for the Medal of Honor. It sounds to me as if you earned it the hard way, Lamprey. I'm proud to call you a fellow Mainiac."

"Thanks, Colonel. Coming from you it means a lot. I don't know what I'm going to do. It took a while, but I accepted the loss of my left arm. That decision was an accomplished fact before I landed the helicopter, but the leg… I prayed so hard to keep it. The doctors said that gangrene had set in and was threatening my life. It had to be removed immediately. I haven't come to grips with it yet. I'm trying, but it seems so damned unfair."

"My daughter Cera also tells me that you and I share an alumni, the University of Maine at Orono."

"Yes, I guess I did tell her that. She's a nice girl. The minute she walked into the ward morale increased a lot."

"What did you do before the war, John?"

"I was a high school math teacher."

"That sounds like a noble endeavor to pursue after the Army fixes you up. I'm not trying to belittle your losses, they're substantial, but they could have been worse. We all have to remember that and not get pulled too deeply in the self-pity routine. They'll be fitting you with an artificial leg and arm. The therapy associated with mastering them will be difficult and time consuming. Once it's over, you'll be able to lead a reasonably normal life teaching school again."

"Nobody wants a cripple teaching kids…," John answered bitterly.

"Cut the crap, John. You know better than that. If anyone objects, ignore them, for they're not worth the energy. Sure, you'll have some limitations, but you're alive and mentally alert. Some veterans never survive the trauma of war and spend the rest of their lives sitting in a chair where they have to be spoon fed every meal and spend every night and day staring at untold horrors that never set them free. You've got some buddies in here that are going home under some pretty pathetic restrictions," Troy continued. "One more thing, John. No one will ever be able to call you a cripple and make it stick unless you think it yourself. You're not a cripple, you're a wounded American soldier wearing the Medal of Honor sash. The whole world respects that Son, and don't forget it!"

John took Troy's right hand in his and squeezed it. "I'm glad you stopped by, Sir. I think the thing I worry the most about is how my family and girlfriend are going to receive me and handle the reality. I don't want them to ignore my injuries as if nothing happened. Time will tell I guess."

"That's the spirit. Sometimes the uniform we wear asks a lot from us. Some individuals sacrifice more than others. I don't have any answer for that. Well, I've been lecturing enough. You look as if you could use some rest right now. Don't let those bad thoughts get you down. Give 'em hell, John. See you around."

"Thanks, Colonel."

Troy had insisted in taking his meals in the hospital cafeteria once he was able to use a wheelchair. He and Cera filled their trays with macaroni and cheese and ham, and they took a seat at a table near a window where they could look out at the mountains to the East.

"I had a talk with John Lamprey," Troy mentioned as they were eating. "I think he's going to be all right. Every injured veteran goes through a period where they view the world as full of obstacles. Self-pity is the first step in acceptance of the situation one is faced with. It helps to develop the resolve necessary to take on the world on its terms. Every person has their unique way of doing that. John has got a lot of strength. He was a high school teacher before going into the Army," Troy related to Cera.

"I'm glad you two talked. He looked so alone and dejected. I wasn't surprised to learn that he was a teacher. I could picture him being one. Incidentally, I've been meaning to ask you something, Dad," said Cera hesitantly.

"What is it, Cera?" Troy asked, turning to look at her.

"Twice I've heard you say the same name in your sleep. Once you said 'Gail, no!' as if you were upset about something. Dad, who was Gail? Do I know her or is that something I don't need to know?"

Troy heard the words and avoided the analytical stare she was giving him. "It was a person I knew during World War Two a long time before I met your mother."

"Was she special, Dad?"

"Cera, my dear girl," replied Troy, thankful that she could not read his mind. He was hesitant to share all that transpired between him and Gail and continued: "It was a time when the whole world was tearing itself apart. I was a frightened young soldier in a strange land half way around the world. Gail was a nurse that helped me recover from wounds I received in Italy."

"I never knew that you were wounded in that war," said Cera, realizing that she had found a part of her father's life that he had kept to himself. He was uncomfortable with the conversation. She saw that same far-away look in his deep-set eyes that the family had occasionally experienced.

Gail, and all that she represented, was a part of life that he was reluctant to share with his beloved daughter or anyone else. It uniquely belonged to him alone. No one could ever understand the depth or longevity of the feelings he held for Gail Malone. Cera saw the conflict taking place within her father and regretted the question.

"I'm sorry, Dad. I didn't mean to pry and I withdraw the inquiry. I was out of line. Forgive me," she cried, touching his arm.

How could he tell Cera, who was not there, what it was like when fear was a dominant emotion in everyone's lives? Within that horrific scene, he saw Gail as an oasis of serenity and calm rationality. She brought meaning and definition to his world and did it by being herself. Caring, generous, courageous, and fragile, she was the embodiment of all that was clean and right with the world. She held a promise of what the future could bring. If a person had not breathed the air filled with pungent smoke and the smell of cordite and gunpowder, they could not know what it was like. If they had not experienced the terror and felt the angst of the period, they could never know. It seemed as if mankind was destroying itself and he was a part of the destruction force.

Troy's iron will was not strong enough to hold back the tears that such memories always produced. Cera saw the pain he bore in silence and was frightened that she had gone too far with her questioning.

"Forgive me, Father," she cried, jumping out of her seat to hold him in her arms. "I had no right… I'm so sorry. How insensitive it was of me!"

Troy loved Cera with all his heart and he knew that her question was a manifestation of the inquisitive side of her nature. It was free of malice and vindictiveness. He owed her some kind of explanation without telling all.

"You have a talent for asking questions that hit the right buttons, Cera," Troy kissed her on the forehead and wiped his eyes. She took her chair and held his hands as he collected his thoughts. "The name Gail has no meaning to you or anyone else in the family. I can't tell you explicitly what you asked, Honey. I simply would not know how to explain it or give it meaning. You would have to have been there to know what it was like and I'm thankful that you'll never be subjected to the terror and fears that were commonplace in that time and place. It was truly a different world."

"I withdraw my question, Dad. I didn't have a right to bring up echoes from the past no matter if they're ugly or precious," Cera said regretfully.

"It was a long time before I met your mother," Troy continued, looking into the past with that same stare they knew so well. "The war was as much an emotion as it has an era of history. It was my baptism of combat. I was wounded in Italy. Combat was not what I had imagined it to be, or what the textbooks describe. I was a naive young country boy from the Maine woods until I came face to face with reality. Combat has its own smell and feel. Violent death leaves a lasting impression on those who see it close up. Anything which helps to remove that image is desperately sought after. A brief moment of denial can mean the difference between sanity and mental collapse. I'm not describing it very well." Troy paused to catch his breath. "Let me say this, my dear child. At that time of my life, the Gail you refer to, gave me the gift of hope for the future, when hope was a very scarce and precious commodity. You don't need to know any more than that and I'm not prepared to elaborate."

Chapter Seven

"Thanks, Dad," said Cera, filled with pride and admiration for his decency and honesty. "Karen and I have always known that there was a part of you that was left unspoken. Over the years we've seen that look on your face we never dared to question. It was a forlorn look that never lasted too long, but, for a moment, it held you captive. Those who loved you saw it clearly."

"You're a perceptive child, Cera. I didn't realize that my reflections were so evident. I'm not trying to be deceptive or secret, and I'm not trying to hide anything I'm ashamed of. It's simply too private right now, Honey. Can you appreciate that?"

"Completely, Daddy. Remind me to tell you that I love you. Mother must be out of her mind to want to move out of a marriage with you," she replied with a deep sigh.

Troy told her that the doctors were planning on moving him to the Presidio at San Francisco. She was given clearance to accompany him on a Military Air Transport plane. Two weeks later, Cera made daily rounds to the soldiers in the wards. The night before they left Schofield Barracks, Cera stopped to visit with John Lamprey.

"We'll be leaving in the morning," explained Cera. "I wanted to say good-bye and wish you well. Hopefully, you'll be going to the mainland soon, too. You look much better than the first time we talked. I'm glad to see that you're making progress. Good luck to you."

"Thanks, Miss Hansen. It's been nice having you around here. You and your Dad have helped me a lot. I appreciate your concern. They're preparing me for a new leg and arm. I'm determined to make them work for me."

"That's the spirit. The future has the potential of being anything we want it to be. As long as we have positive thoughts. It should be a glorious adventure," replied Cera.

"You have a nice way of defining complicated situations. I believe you're going to be successful as a journalist. Good luck to you, Miss Hansen. It has been nice."

"Maybe when Dad gets back up to Maine, we'll see you again," suggested Cera.

"That would be great. I know that I'm going to use the Togus Veteran's Hospital to guide me through the latter stages of therapy. I've already been promised that move. If you want, I could give you my mother's address. My father was killed in action in World War Two." He wrote his address on a piece of tablet paper and passed it to Cera.

"Thanks," said Cera checking the address: Mrs. Lorraine Lamprey, 266 Mountain Road, Westville, Me. "Well, until we meet in Maine sometime, the best of luck to you. You and the other soldiers in this hospital have given me a chance to come face to face with courage and hope. It has been an inspiration to me." Cera leaned over and gently kissed him on the cheek. "You take care soldier."

Returning to the Presidio was like coming home to Troy and Cera. Over the years, he had been posted there several times and been a frequent overnight transient to and from posts all over the world. It is one of the most attractive military posts in the country. Troy had slept most of the way from Hawaii so he was in good spirits by the time they landed in California.

Beth and Karen were on hand to welcome them at the hospital. When Beth saw him being wheeled into the reception center her heart beat faster. The man returning from the war bore little resemblance to the man she had said good-bye to a year ago. Troy's hair was prematurely gray, but the thing that grabbed her like a physical blow were his eyes. They once sparkled with brightness, now they were replaced by a dull gray stare from deeply set eye sockets. When he saw them they lightened up some, but they still reflected the horror he had seen.

Beth embraced him and cried openly. "I'm glad you've come home to us, Troy," she said emotionally.

Karen too was shaken when she saw her father. She hugged him and wept unashamedly on his shoulder. "It's been a long time since I hugged my Dad. Thank God the wars are behind us."

"It's nice to be home," Troy admitted. "How's the expectant mother doing?"

"I'm feeling fine, Daddy. If it's a boy we want to name him after you," she said, wiping the tears away.

"I'll be a proud grandfather, Karen. You take good care of yourself and that little one."

The hospital medical team responsible for Troy interrupted the gathering to announce that they wanted to bring him into the examination room to check him. Troy waved triumphantly to his family as he was being wheeled away. In the excitement of seeing Troy in a wheelchair, Cera was overlooked.

"Oh, Cera," exclaimed her Mother, reaching for her with outstretched arms. "You look wonderful my dear. I'm glad you went to Hawaii to be with your father."

"Me too, Sis," added Karen.

"He looks better than when I first saw him. He seemed to perk up as soon as I got there. I think he had given up."

Cera went home with Karen and her mother. It had been almost a year since they had seen each other. She told them how school was going and that there was nobody "special" in her life, and that she was enjoying the college experience. That next morning, Beth told the girls that she wanted to be alone with their father and left for the Presidio.

"She should spend some time with him," remarked Cera. "She should have done that the minute he arrived in Hawaii."

"Maybe," answered Karen. "She's been very nervous about his homecoming."

"Why Karen?"

"I believe they're heading for a divorce," replied Karen.

"That's not news. They've been on a collision course for years," cried Cera excitedly. "Karen, you and I have been close all through the years. I'm awfully glad to learn that you're pregnant. Tell me honestly. Just what's behind Mom's sudden urge to be free and independent?"

"She'd kill me if I told you," Karen shouted.

55

"I'll kill you if you don't, Karen," screamed Cera. "Look I promise to never divulge anything you may tell me. I simply want to know what in hell is going on with this family!"

"You swear."

"You know I'll keep my word. Does mom have someone else?" asked Cera, holding her breath.

"Yes," replied Karen relieved to be free of the burdensome knowledge.

"That explains everything. I think Dad knows too. He just wants to avoid a nasty battle for our sake. He's going back to Maine you know. I'm going back with him. Someone has got to look after him."

"I think it's for the best, Cera" admitted Karen. "I'm glad we had a chance to talk. I've been feeling that I was part of a monstrous conspiracy to deceive. Mom has been seeing a lawyer in the same town where we went to high school. Evidently it's been going on for a few years. I've been sick about it. I learned about it when my husband Ken was out on a fishing trip one weekend and he saw the two of them together. I'm sorry to have to tell you the sordid news. Poor dad, he deserved better than what he got from mother. His career kept him away from us a lot, but no one had a more caring and loving father than you and me. I'm so proud of him and always have been."

"Did you know that he was awarded the Distinguished Service Cross in Vietnam?" announced Cera.

"No, his modesty would keep him from telling us about it," Karen replied, serving Cera a cup of coffee.

"He didn't tell me either. I learned of it from an ROTC instructor at school in Durham. Thanks for the coffee. It tastes good. You have that healthy glow everyone talks about pregnant mothers having. You're lovelier than ever. I love my big sister."

"And I love you, too, Cera," cried Karen, giving her a hug. For the rest of the day they visited, giggled, and gossiped over old times.

Beth visited Troy at the hospital with the intention of settling things between them. He was sitting in a wheel chair shaving himself when she walked into the room. He was dressed in a hospital johnny draped over his shoulders.

"Good morning, Beth," Troy greeted her enthusiastically. It had been over a year since they had seen each other. "Where are the girls?"

"I left them behind. You and I have got to talk and I don't want them to be a part of what we have to say," said Beth defiantly.

"I'm listening, Beth, but before you continue permit me to make a statement. I can't prove it, but in my gut I know that you've been unfaithful to our vows. I don't want to hear any crap about following one's dreams or incompatibility. It's all a lot of deception and smoke screens for the real reason and we both know what that is. So don't feed me anymore pabulum."

"I didn't want this visit to become uncivil or nasty…"

"What did you expect, Beth, tea and roses?" Troy exclaimed angrily.

"I came here with the intention of telling you that I want a divorce. If you agree, what do you think the terms should be?"

"That's what I like about you Beth, all business and to the point when the baloney is stripped away." Troy found it hard to believe that he and Beth were having this conversation. He knew that it was inevitable, but now that they were having it, the hurt was greater than he had expected. "As far as I'm concerned you can have the divorce. The sooner the better. Your charade has been going on for too long as it is."

"I agree."

"As for terms, I'm going back to Maine just as soon as the Army will let me go. You can have the cottage here in California provided the girls can share it whenever they want. I'd appreciate it if you'd pack my personal stuff at the cottage and ship it to me care of General Delivery in Monson. If you fail to do that I'll void my agreement to divorce and take you to court on grounds of unfaithfulness," Troy threatened with a calmness in his voice that he did not feel inside.

"I'll do it right away," Beth agreed, feeling guilty.

"I'm not so much interested in my clothes at the cottage as I am with my Army records, photo albums, and personal gifts from the girls that I've collected over the years. The rest you can burn or give to the Salvation Army. Oh yes, one more item. You may keep the Ambassador automobile. It's registered in your name anyway. Whatever you have in the savings and checking account you may keep, but my Army retirement, savings accounts, and bonds that are in my name remain my property. That's all I have to say about the situation."

"It's better than I expected and more than I deserve, Troy. Thank you for your sense of fairness. You may find it hard to believe that I don't take this route lightly."

"I'm sure that somewhere in that pretty head of yours there's the same girl that I married. She would be disgusted with this sad turn of events. I've seen it coming and now that we've agreed on the terms, I'm relieved. Over the years you were successful in making me feel guilty for the career I chose. You'll never make me feel that way again. By the way, I know that the only reason you came to see me was to get an approval for a divorce. I should tell you, in case you're interested, that I'll be able to get around with my leg. Thanks for being so considerate and asking how I was doing." Troy could not resist the sarcastic remarks.

"Troy..."

"Good-bye, Beth," Troy said, wheeling his chair down the ward away from her. She exited the hospital in an angry rush.

Within hours of his altercation with Beth, Troy was insisting on being transferred to a facility north of Boston. He suggested the Veteran's Administration Hospital in Togus, Maine. His leg was healing well and he saw no reason to take up room at the prestigious Presidio Hospital. The administration essentially agreed with him. Twenty-four hours later, he and Cera were flying east in a MATS plane for the Naval Air Station at Brunswick, Maine. The last thing Troy did before leaving was to hire a lawyer to start divorce proceedings and to withdraw the stocks and bonds in his name from their security box at a bank in San Francisco. Cera picked up the documents for her father just before they left California.

The swiftness and decisiveness of his moves shocked Cera and Karen. Part of it was his anger at being deceived for so long and being played for a chump. When he thought of how she used him while he was in combat, a powerful rage dictated his moves. Troy wanted out from California and all that it represented, saddened that he had to put the girls in the middle of the volatile separation and divorce, but he was anxious to drop the curtain on that part of his life.

Before he left the Presidio, Troy had a long talk with an old friend, General Wayne, who worked in the Presidio Area Headquarters Command. Troy asked him to be certain that Beth does not touch the retirement accounts or the disability payments due him. General Wayne assured Troy that she could not get them in any way except if he died. Troy had him put the girls as his beneficiary and to remove Beth's name from all insurance accounts.

When Cera and Troy boarded the plane for Maine there was an air of uncertainty between them. A part of Troy was having second thoughts. He may have been too hasty in his actions, but as the miles between the plane and California increased, Troy felt a warm sensation of being cleansed of the worry and suspicion that had been a part of his life for the past two years. The trip to Maine was symbolic of his flight from deceit and unfaithfulness. The rejection still hurt his pride, but the firmness of his resolution to leave without undue regrets made the return to his roots a victorious endeavor.

Cera was uncharacteristically quiet during the flight. She was concerned that Troy was coming to Maine with no destination except the Togus VA Hospital. Troy sensed her discomfort and reached out to squeeze her hand.

"Things will work out, Cera. You'll see. I regret doing this to you and Karen. Your mother has given you girls an example of motherhood conduct that leaves a lot to be desired. I don't intend to bash your mother over what has taken place. She'll always be your mother and you should love her no matter what she has done. It was not intended to hurt you or Karen. She loves and needs you perhaps now more than ever. I bear some responsibility in the break-up of the marriage. I could have taken a job and been home more often like most dads. I chose not to and am willing to accept that consequence."

"Don't be hard on yourself, Daddy. It looks to me as if the two of you were never looking for the same thing. First you pulled the wagon, then Mom pulled it, but rarely did the two of you pull in unison as a team. The marriage was destined to fail. I'm not blaming either of you. I love you both."

"That's the spirit. I have something for you to do as soon as we arrive at Augusta. I want you to go to the nearest Jeep dealer and buy a brand new Jeep Wagoneer with an automatic transmission."

"Have you checked them out, Dad?" she asked, excited about the project.

"Yes, I tried one that an old friend purchased a year or so back. It impressed me. The auto magazines rave about it. It's got enough truck in it to be sturdy and last a long time and enough auto to be comfortable. A perfect blend. They're a four door station wagon with four wheel drive. Perfect for Maine driving conditions. Kaiser has recently been bought out by American Motors. They'll do a good job with the Jeep line of vehicles."

"You're enthused about this aren't you?" It was pleasing for her to see something that animated him. She thought the move to Maine was already taking on a new and positive tone.

"Sure," he answered pressing a check book into her hands. "There are two things I want you to do as soon as we arrive, Cera. Open up an account for you and I as joint tenants at a bank in Augusta with branches throughout the State. Here's a certified check for $100,000.00."

"Dad!"

He placed a finger to her lips asking her to control herself and listen carefully. He talked in a whisper so that no one could hear. "I've signed the check. Deposit it in a checking account for you and I. Then use your best dickering skills to purchase a 1970 Jeep Wagoneer with automatic transmission and four wheel drive. Pick out the color you like the best. We don't need a lot of fancy options. I should warn you that tan or silver colors are absolutely out. Anything else is okay with me. You can do that, Cera. I wouldn't have asked if I thought differently."

"I've never seen that kind of money in my life, Dad," she declared with an impish gleam in her eye. "What would you say if I skipped town and took the money with me?"

"I'd find you sooner or later," Troy laughed. "This is the first day of our big adventure, Cera. You said you would come to Maine with me. What do you say now?"

"I'm discovering a father that is capable of making important decisions in a short period of time. I'm also thinking that I may have to keep a sharp watch over you."

They laughed and hugged each other. The unknown and a new tomorrow was waiting for them. All they had to do was embrace the future.

Chapter Eight

The Togus Veteran's Administration Hospital began intense therapy on his leg as soon as he arrived. The cast was removed and a lightweight metal tubular brace was fabricated to hold the bones in his leg in alignment until the fractured sections were completely healed. At first he was able to walk with crutches, but he disliked the awkwardness and adamantly rejected them. He was determined to walk with the assistance of a cane while wearing the brace. If it became a permanent part of his recovery, he could accept it and be thankful for the ability to walk, but crutches were definitely out as far as he was concerned.

Cera had rented a room at a small inn within walking distance of the hospital. While Troy was involved in the therapy routine, Cera was carrying out his request to purchase a Jeep Wagoneer. She fell in love with the vehicle the first time she took one for a test drive. It was a deep maroon exterior with gray and maroon cloth seats. The vehicle gave her freedom of movement, a luxury she had not had since she started school. She explored sections of central Maine with a few excursions to the coast.

One day, while Cera and Troy were in the activity room playing cribbage, an orderly told Troy that the chief surgeon wanted to see him. He excused himself and followed the orderly to the doctor's office.

"I wanted to talk to you, Colonel Hansen, about your recovery schedule," stated Doctor Kelly.

"Bad news, Doctor?" questioned Troy, leaning on his cane.

"Please sit down, Colonel. I've received your complete medical records and information pertaining to your career in the Army. The Army is leaving the decisions to me whether or not you should be medically discharged. It's a little premature to make a full evaluation. However, it's something that should be discussed if for no other reason than for you to plan for the future."

"With the knowledge you have on my leg up to this time, Doctor Kelly, what's your best guess?"

"Unless I see a lot of improvement when the brace is removed and your cane is thrown away, I'd have to sign your discharge papers."

"I see."

"You must have known that it was a possibility, Colonel."

"I've considered it. My opinion has never been confirmed by a doctor before. It's not an easy conclusion to adjust to, but I will be ready to enter civilian life if that's forced on me."

"You've had a distinguished career in the Army, Colonel. Twenty-eight years and three wars is a major commitment for any man. If you want, I'll sign your papers any day you ask for it. Other than the leg, you're in excellent health and better condition than many your age. I'll leave the ultimate decision to you. That does not mean that I will allow you to return to active status in the Army if I believe your leg is questionable for active campaigning. I don't believe you'd want it any other way."

"I appreciate your honest evaluation, Doctor. How long will it take for my leg to heal completely?"

"By the end of the summer. We don't need to keep you here. As a matter of a fact you're free to leave any time you desire. You can use us as a walk-in outpatient clinic twice a week for the next month. The therapy department will give you exercise routines that will strengthen your leg. You don't need confinement to do that."

"If that's the case, I'm going to check out today and visit friends in the Moosehead Lake area. My daughter will drive me. If you don't mind, Doctor, I'd like to postpone my decision to the end of summer. The first chance I've got, I'm going fishing," explained Troy, enthused about having the summer to do what he wanted without restrictions.

"You do that, Colonel, and good luck to you. You've earned the right to enjoy the summer."

"C'mon Cera, we're getting out of here right now," Troy exclaimed to Cera who was waiting for him in the corridor.

"Where are we going?"

"Anywhere. You're the chauffeur," grinned Troy. "I'll go along for the ride. I haven't ridden in our new vehicle yet. I'll collect my things and we'll do what was a popular saying during the Korean War. We'll pull a Hank Snow and 'Move On'."

Her father's enthusiasm was contagious. Cera smiled and gave him a hug. "I'll help you pack then we'll stop at the inn to pick up my stuff. This is exciting, Dad. Back at Pearl Harbor I was afraid that this kind of opportunity would never present itself."

While Cera was collecting her things at the inn, Troy placed a phone call to Ashley Cooper at Kokadjo. He had called her when he first arrived at Togus and had promised to visit her on his first trip away from the hospital.

"Hello," answered a soft melodious voice.

"Hello, Ashley. This is Troy Hansen."

"It's nice to hear from you, Troy. How are you doing? I've been praying for you ever since your daughter, Cera, visited me."

"I'd like to sit down and talk with you about your proposal. Cera can drive me there as soon as we hang up," suggested Troy optimistically.

"That'll be fine. I'll look forward to seeing you and Cera again. Why don't you plan on staying for a while? It'll be nice to have an old friend for company."

"Since you put it that way we can't refuse, Ashley. We'll be there as soon as we can. Maybe three hours."

"From Augusta that will be about right. I'll have something to eat. I have a couple of fresh trout I caught from the dock this morning."

"Ashley, there's nothing I'd like any more than fresh trout. I'll be counting the miles until we get there."

"Tell Cera to drive carefully."

"Thank you, Ashley." Troy hung up and smiled. She was some lady! An air of serenity and harmony emanated from the gracious lady of the North Woods. How lucky her people will be if she does go back to work for their welfare.

Cera guided the powerful V/8 engine-equipped Wagoneer onto the freeway in Augusta. She was relaxed and confident behind the wheel. Troy was like a kid with a new toy getting out of school early.

"This is great," he said checking the instrument cluster. "Don't you like the smell of a new car?"

"I love this vehicle, Dad. I think you made a wise choice. It has a lot of pep and handles well. I have a secure feel behind the wheel."

"The ride is better than I expected. It's still a little firmer than a regular automobile. That's because of the straight springs under the front end."

"Maybe I'll try it after we get to Ashley's place. The automatic transmission makes it easier for someone with a bum leg to drive."

"I've been thinking, Dad. This would be a great vehicle to take back to school this September," suggested Cera, testing the waters of opportunity.

"Dream on kid," Troy laughed with her. "Nice try. We'll see what comes this September. I'm not promising a thing."

"No harm in asking."

Ashley Cooper hung up the phone and walked out on the porch overlooking the Lake of Three Sorrows. It was a pleasant warm June day. The sun was bright and the sky was an azure blue from horizon to horizon without a cloud in sight. She sat in a rocking chair and sighed. It was lonely for her in this small piece of paradise she had shared with her husband, Dale, and her beloved daughter, Heather. Memories from the past were an important part of her life. Even now, twenty-six years after her death, she could hear Heather's voice. Occasionally she heard the piano playing and looked to see if she was there. The sounds that came from her treasured memory were clear and distinct, just as if Heather was alive. Tears came easily when she remembered how close Heather and Dale had been.

Ashley had given a lot of thought about the proposal she was going to make to Troy Hansen. She had contemplated passing it on to someone in her native village or to friends in the area. None of those choices seemed to "fit" as nicely as Troy and his family. Cera's visit earlier in the spring was an enjoyable one. She reminded Ashley of Heather. The proud way she carried herself and confronted the world head on with that independent attitude the two young ladies shared.

Ashley rechecked the guest bedroom again to be certain it was ready to receive company. She thought that Cera could sleep in the loft above the great room where she had slept during her last visit in the Spring. The loft had been a favorite for Heather, too. Dale and Ashley had used it on occasion when they were younger. She saw her dead husband everywhere in the cabin. The memories were priceless treasures, but the immediacy of his presence reminded her of his passing and she was having trouble letting go. Dale would not want her to sit and mourn for the rest of her life, but she loved him without reservation, and it was impossible to not remember how it had been.

An opportunity to serve her people in a constructive manner meant a lot to her. She quickly accepted the offer as a nurse at the infirmary in her native village. Dale would approve and be proud of her.

Later, that same afternoon, Cera turned the Wagoneer into the long gravel driveway leading to the cabin on the Lake of Three Sorrows. It was like coming home to Troy. Nothing had changed as he remembered it. They saw Ashley sitting in a rocker on the porch. When she saw the Wagoneer Ashley stepped down from the porch to greet them. She was still a beautiful woman. Her bronze skin and high cheek bones reflected her Cree heritage. Her white hair, cut short just below the ear, blew in the wind as she ran towards them. Tall and regal in bearing, Ashley seemed to glide across the ground.

"You've made good time. I'm so glad to see both of you," she exclaimed, without a trace of being out of breath from the dash to the automobile.

Cera was the first to grab her in a warm embrace. "It's nice to be here again, Mrs. Cooper."

Ashley turned to look at Troy. She saw what was in his eyes. She had seen the same look in her Dale. She opened her arms to receive him. "We've got to make you forget what those eyes have seen my dear friend. Welcome to our home. It's been a long time."

"You're right, Ashley. It has been too long. I didn't know about Dale's passing until Cera told me. I'll miss his gentle ways. You're as lovely as ever. Time has been generous to you, Ashley."

The minute Troy entered the familiar cabin he was greeted by a scent he rarely encountered anywhere else in the world. The subtle aroma of the heliotrope family of flowers. He looked on the desk near the fireplace for the familiar reddish-purple Bloodstone flower. It had grown some as he remembered. It was nice to acknowledge those small things that helped make a house a home.

Cera volunteered to help Ashley prepare supper. Troy noted that the fire was started in the charcoal grill in front of the porch. Cera placed a chair near the grill so that her father could tend the trout over the glowing coals. He readily accepted the assignment. One of Ashley's great charms was her ability to convey to others how important they were to her. Troy was so thrilled to be there that he had missed a two-toned green Wagoneer a couple of years old parked beside the woodshed at the rear of the cabin.

"How do you like your Wagoneer, Ashley?"

She came to the porch to answer him. "When Dale and I first married, we tried several makes and models of vehicles. After the war, Dale was the first in the area to purchase one of those early square box-like Jeep station wagons. Their four-wheel-drive capabilities made living here year-round much easier. They gave us a secure feeling if we had to get out in severe weather. This is my second Wagoneer and I can't praise it enough. We've had Jeep vehicles since 1946. Yours is a pretty color."

"I haven't driven it yet but it goes over the road nicely."

"They're fun to drive. You sit up higher than a car and can see around you better. Potatoes and green peas are ready when you've got the trout browned to suit your taste."

"Coming right up."

The subject of selling the place was brought up while they were eating. Ashley told Troy that she felt comfortable selling it to him if he was interested. She had had the place appraised. They came up with the same figure the Town had used for tax valuation. She would sell it for fifteen thousand dollars. It had to be understood that was just for the cabin. All of the land, including the Lake of Three Sorrows, belonged to the Great Northern Paper Company. They had given them a lease of the land for one hundred years. They had renewed the lease in 1933, so there were sixty-seven years left unless it was renewed again. The lease cost ten dollars per year with the provision that employees of GBPC could seek shelter in the cabin in time of emergency if needed. The company looked upon residence in the isolated location as a good safety measure for fire prevention and general land management.

Cera had been listening to Ashley describe the property. She knew what her father's answer was going to be. It already felt more like home to her than the cottage in California.

"If I agree to buy it, Ashley, will you promise to visit as often as you wish? Also, if you ever want it back, or if your venture in Canada does not pan out as expected, then I agree to deed it back to you. Just give me a few days to pack up!"

"No, Troy. That would not be fair to your family, but I appreciate your generosity. I'll be back sometime for a visit. Incidentally how is Beth?" asked Ashley.

"You'll be surprised to know that Beth and I are getting a divorce."

"No! I'm sorry for both of you. Don't tell me the reasons behind it, I don't want to know." Ashley looked at Cera sitting across the table from her. "Your younger daughter has turned into a lovely young lady. I'm sorry for you, Cera, and your sister Karen. I suppose it's easier when you're older, yet, breaking up a marriage is a sad affair."

"Sometimes it's sadder to continue one that has stopped working the way it should," Troy defended his decision and changed the subject. "How soon do you want to make a move, Ashley? I'm out of the hospital on a short furlough."

"It would be easier for me to make the move during these warm summer months. I'll be driving to Lac Saint Jean. The roads are much improved in Canada than when I left years ago. If I had a chance, I'd prefer sooner rather than later. If you're prepared to accept the arrangement we could agree to agree and make the transaction when you or your bank have ascertained that the title is clear and legitimate."

"I have no doubt of that. If you agree. I could give you a check for the amount you ask. You can deposit it and wait for it to clear. That'll give you a chance to have a deed drawn up for the title transfer. I want it understood that you will always be welcome at any time of your choosing, without exception. I'm aware that you have strong emotional attachment to this beautiful place. I would never deprive you of the opportunity to revisit."

"You're a generous man, Troy Hansen. You and my Dale were cut from the same cloth. I know that he would approve of what we are discussing. I really didn't want to sell it to a stranger. I know that Cera and Karen like it here. The times you and your family visited were special for Dale and me. It was nice to hear the laughter of children again."

"Ashley, the purchase of this place is the fulfillment of all my dreams. I'll be able to renew myself and find myself in the solitude of the forest and lake. I've needed that for a long time. The breaking up of our marriage is not all Beth's fault. I've failed the family in important ways by being absent too much, but that's in the past and we have to look forward to the future. I need some time to evaluate where I go from here. I'm beholden to you and Dale for giving me that chance."

"I plan to stay with my father for the rest of the summer until school starts in September," added Cera, pleased with the rapid turn of events.

"You look tired, Troy. If you wish to retire please do so. I've made up the guest room for you. Cera is young enough to negotiate the ladder to the loft," Ashley smiled and placed an arm around Cera. "I'm glad you came with your father."

"You know, Ashley, I think I'll take you up on your offer to retire. May I make a request before I do that?"

"Of course you may."

"Would you please play the piano for us? You play so beautifully," Troy requested.

"If you wish. One of my favorites lately is *Canadian Sunset*. The sun is beginning to dip below the horizon across the lake. It's an appropriate song to end the day."

Ashley took a seat on the bench running her long supple fingers across the keyboard to exercise them and began the popular and beautiful song. She closed her eyes playing with passion and feeling. She wrapped herself in the music and her fingers telegraphed what was in her heart. Troy was correct, she played beautifully, sitting erect and proud.

Cera was moved by her interpretation of the song. When Ashley had finished, Cera leaned down and hugged her. "A beautiful song played by a beautiful lady."

"You flatter me my dear girl. Thank you for your kind thoughts. I'll do one more. It was a favorite for Dale and Heather who played much better than I – *Danny Boy* or *Londonderry Air*."

The haunting strains echoed through the cabin to the still waters of the lake. The majestic spruce trees swayed gently in the soft evening breeze. Troy retired to the guest room as she was playing. It had been a busy day and he was exhausted. The last stanza of the song filled the room and gently faded into silence. Minutes later the lonely cry of loons pierced the still air. Troy felt contentment and peace for the first time in years. He had come home!

Chapter Nine

A week later, Cera and Troy returned to the Lake of Three Sorrows. The legal papers had been processed and a deed duly registered at the County Registry of Deeds. He was officially the owner of the property. Within that period Togus Hospital had been vigorously working and exercising his leg. He still needed the cane to feel secure, but he was making progress, yet, he would have to wear the brace for the rest of the year as an insurance against premature failure and for complete healing of the fracture. He was exuberant with the prognosis, and was prepared to live with the brace even if it became a permanent fixture.

Cera's encouragement and support helped him. Her positive energy rubbed off on him and her playful attitude made the therapy sessions fun. When she wasn't with Troy she was out buying supplies and personal items for the cabin. Her enthusiasm for the place equaled Troy's.

They helped Ashley pack her personal items and clothing in her Wagoneer. It was filled to capacity when they were finished. She was anxious to be on the road, returning to her roots in Canada had been a part of her dream for several years.

"In many ways," she explained in that soft gentle way she had. "This place never belonged to Dale or me. Maybe it will be the same for you, Troy. It really belongs to the spirits of the Indian maiden and her two children. God has chosen to create a sanctuary here where lives are healed and prepared for the fulfillment of their destiny. I hope it is that way for you. Good-bye, dear friend. I leave the Lake of Three Sorrows in good hands."

Ashley promised Cera and Troy that she would be back for an occasional visit. She embraced them on the porch and slowly walked toward the Wagoneer. She turned for one last look at the cabin and the lake. Years of happiness and contentment flashed through her memory. Her eyes briefly filled with tears and an intense loneliness sent a ripple of sadness through her body.

With a quick wave of her hand and a honk on the horn Ashley disappeared from sight down the long driveway.

"There goes a remarkable lady," whispered Troy, feeling that he had just lost something important in his life. "I'll miss her."

Cera placed an arm around her father's waist and gently squeezed him. She heard what he had said to himself and had similar sentiments. The day was important, because it marked a new beginning, not only for Ashley, but for her father. Chills ran up and down her spine as she watched the blue-green water gently lap against the rocky shore. She truly loved the place. It brought an element of order and calm to her soul.

"Well, Cera. What do you think? Have we made the right move?" Troy turned to her. "You seem a little quiet. Is everything all right?"

"I was simply thinking how beautiful this place is. I hope you're going to be as happy here as Ashley and Dale were. I understand what you said about needing a place to find yourself again. I really believe that you've found it, Daddy. I love it here. It's difficult to describe, but there's an energy here that encompasses you and lifts your spirits. Do you feel it?"

"I do, Honey. I knew that you were getting the same perceptions by the expression on your face." Troy sat on the swinging couch on the porch and started to look through the large pouch of mail that had been forwarded from Beth and Karen through the Army Post Office. "Here's a letter to you from John Lamprey."

"Thanks, Dad. I've been wondering how he was getting along." Cera opened the letter and read:

Schofield Barracks Hospital

May 25, 1970

Dear Miss Hansen;

This letter might surprise you. The days and nights here are long and I miss you and your father. What's left of my leg is healing well. I've started therapy and am learning how to manipulate the artificial arm and the leg. It's going to be a while but I'm determined to master their use so that I can minimize my limitations. The advice your Dad gave me has helped a lot. I hope he's doing well. He seemed to perk up as soon as he learned that he was going to the mainland.

I'm going home soon. The President will present the Medal of Honor to me early in June. Afterwards I'm going to the Veteran's Administration Hospital in Togus, Maine where I'll complete my leg and arm therapy. They'll do my final fittings too.

If you care to write to me you may use the Togus address. If I'm not there they'll be able to forward it to me. If you're too busy I understand. I just wanted to thank you for helping me at a time when I needed a comforting word and a friendly smile. You helped me change my attitude towards my injuries, and for that I'll always be grateful.

One day I'm going to walk back into a classroom to teach!

I wish you all the best. Good luck back in school this September.

Yours truly,

John Lamprey,

Warrant Officer, USA

Cera passed the letter to her father. He read it with interest. "He's a brave young man. This country is blessed with many like him. I'm biased, I admit, but some of the best we have wear our country's uniform. I'm proud of John. There was a quiet solidness about him that was reassuring. Are you going to answer him?"

"Yes, I owe him that. I hope we can be friends. I liked his modesty and honesty. He's going to be all right. It won't be easy, but he's the type that will pull it off by sheer will."

"I'd say you read the young man correctly," Troy replied, noting Cera's flushed cheeks. "I've had four different notes from some of my old buddies pertaining to a twenty-five year reunion of World War Two veterans of the Normandy invasion." He pondered the prospects.

"Would Togus approve of you going, Dad?"

"I think so. I'm getting stronger every day. I could continue with my exercises and wear my brace day and night so as to eliminate any complications."

"Are you prepared to revisit old battlefields?" Cera asked, concerned that it may not be a good time for him to review the old echoes he hears so frequently. She had read that old wounds and feelings can be reopened at such occasions. With his present fragile emotional condition it might be too much.

"At some time I need to go back. Would you like to go with me, Cera?"

"If you really think that you should, I wouldn't want to be in the way."

"You could never be that, Cera. Maybe you'll be able to better understand me if you see some of the places I've been."

"I'd like that, Dad. I already have a passport," she added.

"That's great, then we'll set it in motion. My old regiment is meeting in England before we cross over the English Channel to France. It'll be an education for you. I'm glad that you can share the trip with me." Troy looked at his younger daughter sitting on the porch in a rocking chair with her legs curled up under her. "You know, I'm going to get a fish pole out of the woodshed and sink a line off the dock. Maybe I can catch supper."

"I'm going to write a letter to John Lamprey," Cera replied. She collected a notepad and her prized Parker '51 fountain pen and returned to the swing.

Lake of Three Sorrows

Kokadjo, Maine

June 5, 1970

Dear John,

I received your letter today and was glad to hear from you. The general tone of the letter was positive and I am proud of the progress you are making with the therapy and the healthy mental adjustments you seem to have made. You've already taken a giant step towards recovery.

My father and I are now at a place north of Moosehead Lake. Dad signed papers today for the property. So far I enjoy the solitude and serenity of being on the edge of the great Maine wilderness.

Dad is going through therapy at Togus. Maybe we'll meet you there. I'm excited to learn that the President is going to award the Medal of Honor to you at the Oval office in the White House. Your family must be proud of you, too.

This year is the 25th anniversary of the end of World War Two. Dad and I are going to England and Normandy for the reunion. I'm looking forward to seeing firsthand what my Father's generation went through. I'm not sure how long we'll be gone. When we return he'll definitely touch base at Togus.

Keep thinking positive about the future, John. Any soldier who has the courage that a MOH recognizes, can conquer anything he sets his heart and mind to. Best of luck. Hope to see you soon.

A friend,

Cera Hansen

Troy caught two large trout and dressed them for supper. Later, they made arrangements with the travel agency handling the reunion for his regiment and got ready to leave for Portland first thing in the morning.

75

That evening, Troy was powerless to block the images and sounds that ran through his mind. Cera would be surprised if she knew how often he thought about Gail. He knew more than anyone that it was dangerous to dwell on the past when nothing can be changed. There was more to it than a yearning to be with Gail. He had loved a brave nurse that had touched his heart at a time when the future was uncertain. Love and peace of mind were so intense it influenced everything he did. It had shielded him from the fear and trauma of combat as if she had encased him in an impenetrable cocoon. She had empowered him to be more than he was capable of being on his own, and that was an important product of their love for each other. Troy was anxious to return to Europe. Maybe, just maybe, he could close that chapter of his life and set free the memories that continued to shackle him.

He was fifty years old. Two thirds of his life had passed beyond recall. The remaining one third was whatever he wanted it to be, and he was determined to give it some meaning beyond the bittersweet memories. The reunion was a good place to start the healing process.

* * *

Later that night, Troy relived the day he and Gail had agreed to meet at the Wentworth-By-Sea Hotel in Newcastle, New Hampshire one hundred and eighty days after the surrender of Germany. On November 4, 1945 he had driven to the hotel and sat on the wide veranda for hours staring at the ocean. He knew that it would hurt, yet, he did it anyway as a tribute to what might have been. People walked in and out of the busy hotel. The couples had accentuated the fact that he was alone, accompanied only by memories. The loneliness was overpowering. It had been a cool fall day and the damp breeze off the ocean was chilling.

Troy left the hotel and drove to Buzzard's Bay, Massachusetts where Gail had lived, checking at the local library for the High School Yearbooks. She had graduated in 1938. When he last saw her in 1944, she had not changed much from her graduation picture. She had been active in school affairs and was praised for her piano playing skills. He had never heard her talk about that. There had been a fresh wholesomeness about her that had never changed.

He checked the local phone book at a restaurant in the middle of the town and found a listing for a Mr. and Mrs. Henry Malone. He was tempted to call but restrained himself. A call from him could only stir up painful memories, so he reluctantly hung up the phone. Troy ate dinner at the restaurant recalling that the cashier had talked to him about the ending of the war and how all of the men were coming home at last.

* * *

Troy woke from his reverie to the aroma of coffee percolating. He climbed out of bed and saw Cera sitting at the table drinking coffee and eating toast with peanut butter.

"Good morning, Cera. That coffee does smell good," he declared. "How long have you been up?"

"A couple of hours. Would you like a couple of eggs and some toast?" Cera was already dressed for the trip.

"If you want to be the chef, I like mine scrambled. I'll slip in the bathroom to shower and shave while you do that."

"Are you excited about the trip, Dad?" He looked a little tired to her. It was important that he not push himself too far too fast.

"Yes, it'll be good to see some of the old gang. We went through quite a lot together. We were part of the Army's First Infantry Division. Whenever I think of what our soldier-citizens did I swell with pride. They met the best the world had seen up 'til that time, the German Army, a professional, well-equipped, well-led force. When you've fought them you know that you're up against the first team."

Cera kissed him on the cheek and directed him towards the bathroom. "We don't have that much time, Dad. Breakfast will be ready when you are."

After breakfast, Cera packed their bags in the Wagoneer. "Gee, I really like the Jeep, Dad. They're quite popular in Maine I notice."

"The winters are severe in this part of northern Maine. A lot of people don't realize it but we're further north than

Montreal. The winters test a vehicle to the limit. The four-wheel-drive feature will add to our security."

"I've got a thermos of coffee and some sandwiches already packed for the flight. We should get going, Dad."

"You're as bad as a first sergeant I once had," grinned Troy. "It's going to be fun making this trip with you, Cera. Maybe I haven't told you girls as often as I should, but regardless of the differences between your mother and me, you two girls have always been the joy of my life. Your happiness means more to me than anything in the world."

"You've shown your love time after time over the years. Here we are leaving on a short trip and I already feel sad about leaving this place. It kind of attaches itself to you doesn't it?"

"That's for sure. Leaving will be easy knowing that it's waiting for our return. I'm all set. You warm up the Wagoneer and I'll lock up behind us."

Ten hours later, Cera and Troy landed at Heathrow, the large London Airport. They took a cab to one of the hotels under contract to the travel agency that had sponsored the tour. For the next two days hundreds of veterans arrived from the United States and joined in the organized tours to various installations along the coastal region of England where most of the men had stayed in barracks while waiting for the invasion to take place.

It was a different London than Troy remembered. The bombed out sections of the city had been rebuilt and cars and trucks whipped around the city with abandon. During the war years, traffic was primarily of military vehicles and large numbers of bicycles. Cera was wide-eyed with excitement taking in everything she saw and heard. She was like a little girl when she recognized Big Ben and the London Bridge. Driving on the opposite side of the road still seemed a little weird to Troy. He told Cera that Americans really had to concentrate on their driving or they'd cause an accident when they forgot.

The first day was a long and tiring one for Troy. He confided to Cera that he was going to go to bed early. The next day's schedule was a busy one and he wanted to be rested for it. They had requested a small two room suite with a connecting bath and small sitting room.

"Before I do that, what do you say if we eat in the dining room? I'm hungry. Your sandwiches and coffee were a lifesaver on the plane."

"I'm hungry, too. It's located just off the desk reception area. A good meal will help you keep up your strength. Have you seen any familiar faces yet?" asked Cera noting the large number of men and women his age circulating around the hotel.

"None yet. Tomorrow morning, when we meet at the conference room, I expect we'll begin to see some of the men. They'll be passing out name tags then. They'll help to jog fading memories. Twenty-five years have passed and we're no longer young. I'm looking forward to it."

They took a table near the large gas-fired fireplace. It was twice as large as the one in their cabin back home. The fire was warm and cheerful, for the air was damp. As soon as the sun went down a jacket or a sweater felt good. Troy was wearing his uniform. The clerks and waiters that recognized it went out of their way to be hospitable. Cera noted how the American uniform, and the men who wore it were an object of respect. The dining room was rapidly filling to capacity.

Troy sat facing the fireplace. Cera was positioned to his right so that she could see the fire and people as they entered the dining area. She did not feel like a stranger in a foreign land. Most of the people were middle-aged Americans present for the tour.

As a matter of fact, most of the men were sober, even taciturn, returning to the scene where they first experienced bloodshed and horror. For many it was not a reunion but a pilgrimage. Some were bringing their families with them hoping that they would be able to understand what it was like to have been a part of the largest military invasion force the world has ever known. Cera, too, was in that category. Maybe when the tour was over she could appreciate their loss of innocence and their introduction to terror that the battlefield represented.

The reunion gave the rest of the world an opportunity to say: "Thank you for your sacrifice. We can't ever know what it was truly like to be in such intense combat, but we acknowledge that you left a part of your youth, your dreams for the future, and many of your friends and buddies who never went back home." The hardest part of reunions was remembering the large numbers of men buried in shallow graves, struck down in their youth. . .

Chapter Ten

Troy would have known that he was in England when he heard the weak sounding automobile horns on the street outside the hotel. American cars had much higher pitched horns that grabbed your attention. He was filled with high expectations for the trip, and was genuinely anxious to see old buddies he had soldiered with.

In his heart he knew that something else was calling him back to the scene of his life twenty-five years ago. The past few weeks had changed his life completely. Changes from normalcy were the order of the day. A pending divorce from Beth, and ownership of the cabin at Lake of Three Sorrows had altered the dynamics of the question: "Where do I go from here?" He had been asking himself that question for a long time. The answers were not forthcoming until he left Hawaii.

At some time, Troy, also, knew that he would have to look backward on his life to find the right direction for the future. One reason for the trip was obvious. It was imperative that he put to rest that short time he had spent with Gail during the war. Perhaps, he rationalized, a revisit to the familiar places would allow him to turn that page in his life.

The next morning Troy showered and shaved ahead of Cera who had stayed up much of the night reading Cornelius Ryan's, *D-Day*. He emerged from the bathroom checking in a mirror to see that his necktie was straight and his uniform spotless. He was particular about it and saw to it that those in his command followed his example. His ribbons were straight and evenly spaced. He was proud of his Distinguished Service ribbon, but the one he was most proud of was the Combat Infantryman's Badge. He did not deceive himself that when the time came for him to retire from the Army, he would miss the distinction and dedication the uniform represented. He sat in a chair looking out across the city thinking of how it had been twenty-five years ago in wartime London.

Later, Cera came out of the bathroom dressed in a maroon pant suit with a beige blazer. She had a small beret-like hat that sat on her head at a rakish angle.

"You look wonderful, Cera. Are you ready for some breakfast?" asked Troy.

"I'm famished, Dad. You look very distinguished in your uniform this morning. Many of my girlfriends at high school thought you were a handsome man. I was inclined to agree with them."

"With pleasantries like that, let's go out and take on the day," he winked at her.

Cera linked her right arm through his left and walked to the elevator. The lobby was noisy and busy. The dining room was a more relaxing atmosphere with several empty booths and tables. Most of the tourists took meals in their rooms, especially breakfast. Troy ordered scrambled eggs with corned beef and toast and asked for coffee. If they did not have it he was prepared to drink tea. Cera ordered the same thing. They sat at the same table they had the night before. The fire in the fireplace had recently been rekindled and was an interesting focal point for patrons of the dining room.

Part way through their leisurely breakfast, Cera excused herself and went to the ladies rest room. It was a spotless facility with a pleasant clean aroma. She used one of the stalls and was washing her hands at one of the wash stands, when a strange feeling came over her that she was not alone. Looking up at the large mirror in front of her she noticed a middle-aged woman feeling the wall opposite the washstands with her hands. There was a nervous movement to her hands that caught Cera's attention. Her first thought was that it was a weird thing for an adult to do in a restroom. Then she heard a muffled cry come from the woman as if she was frightened.

"Excuse me," announced Cera, walking towards the woman. "Is there anything I can do to help you?" It was a natural thing for her to ask. As she drew closer, it was evident that the woman was extremely agitated.

"Oh, yes," the woman answered in a soft resonant voice. "When I entered the room, I thought I knew where the door was located. Somehow I became disoriented. Now I can't find it and I'm afraid." The lady began to cry. There was an air of desperation about her that touched Cera.

"Come, let me help you," said Cera. "There's a bench right beside us. Please sit down and rest a moment. I'm an American visitor here."

"I knew that the second you began to speak," replied the woman, relieved that someone could help her.

Cera thought she was an attractive lady. Her blonde hair with streaks of gray hung loose about her shoulders. She wore a pair of dark green slacks with a matching blazer over a white blouse with lace around her neck. She was tense and nervous. A small cap with an attached first lieutenant bar was pulled down over her forehead with a short white veil covering her eyes and nose. She wore a dark brown pair of glasses. The name tag she was wearing carried her name as *Ensign G. Malone.*

"I apologize for being a bother," the lady exclaimed. "Normally, I'm not this helpless."

"Come now, you're not a bother to me," replied Cera still holding her hand. "Are you here for the Normandy tours?"

"Yes, my son wanted to come with me. I was a nurse attached to a unit that followed the first wave of troops ashore. Now, I'm not so sure that it was a good idea to return. You're very kind, young lady. May I feel your face so that I can see you? I'm blind."

"Of course, if you wish," answered Cera surprised at the unusual request. There was something about this blind lady and her vulnerability that drew Cera to her. Cera took her hands and placed them on her cheeks. It was an experience she never forgot. Soft caring fingers traced the contours of her eyes, nose, cheeks and mouth.

"You're beautiful. Thank you for helping me. My son is waiting for me outside the door. He'll think something has happened to me. I don't very often lose my orientation when I come into a strange room. Would you please show me to the door?"

"I'd be glad to." Cera held her arm and directed her towards the door, holding it open for her to walk through. Cera followed.

They were met by a tall American soldier, a young second lieutenant about Cera's age. The minute their eyes met Cera thought she had met him before. He looked familiar but she could not place where she had seen him. All of her life she had been in and around Army bases and had met countless numbers of young officers. The name card he was wearing said Second Lieutenant Alan Malone.

"Alan," the lady announced when he took her arm in his. "This young lady has been very kind. I lost my direction in there and she helped me."

"Thank you for assisting my mother," said the soldier. He had dark brown hair and expressive eyes that could praise or chastise at the same time. There was a strong presence about him that got a person's attention. Cera saw how protective he was of his mother without being condescending. She liked that about him.

Cera squeezed her hand and said: "I'm glad I could help, Mrs. Malone."

"Thank you. What is your name?" inquired the lady as an after thought.

"They call me Cera."

"That's a nice name."

"We've got to get along, Mother. Thanks again for helping, Cera," prompted Alan, guiding his mother to a table in the middle of the dining hall.

Cera took her seat at Troy's table. The encounter left her with an unsettled feeling. Her father picked up on it as soon as she sat down.

"Is everything all right, Cera?" he asked. "You look distressed about something." She told him about the chance meeting with the blind lady in the restroom without elaborating on the feelings that accompanied the incident.

Suddenly, a portly, middle-aged man accompanied by two young men hailed Troy from a few tables away. "Captain Troy Hansen," the man exclaimed, approaching their table. "I'd recognize you anywhere. You might not recognize me with this added weight, I'm Sergeant Eli Ford. How nice it is to see you again."

A moment after Sergeant Ford greeted Troy a disturbance took place near the center of the dining room. Several people rushed to assist the lady Cera had met in the restroom. Evidently she had fainted and fell to the floor. Cera saw her Son briskly carrying her out of the hall.

"Sergeant Ford, it's been a while hasn't it? I'm glad you could make the tour." Troy rose to shake hands with the robust Eli Ford, his old company clerk.

"I didn't realize you had stayed in after the war, Sir. That Distinguished Service Cross looks good on you, Colonel. These two youngsters are my sons, James and Harold. I brought them along in the hopes that they would be able to understand what it was like. I don't know about you, Sir, but that last battle we were in before the breakout from the coastal plains was as fierce as I experienced throughout the war. I still remember how some of our buddies died…"

Troy embraced the emotional Sergeant Ford. The only people who could really know what the powerful memories were like, were other veterans of that campaign. They were locked together in a fraternal brotherhood for the rest of their lives. The sergeant's recollections were typical. The tour would give them a chance to say good-bye again to old friends, eighteen and twenty year old buddies they had helped place in body bags.

Sergeant Ford and Troy clung to each other surprised at the intensity of the feelings that gripped them. Cera watched the two sons. They were somewhat embarrassed by the show of feelings. She whispered softly to herself: "You'll never be able to understand, boys. All we can do is appreciate what they experienced across the dark waters of the English Channel on the bloody beaches of Normandy."

"I'm glad to meet you boys. This is my daughter Cera. Your dad was our company clerk. He spent a lot more time in the front lines with a Thompson submachine gun than he did with a typewriter," Troy explained to the young teenagers. "He was one of the best. I hope you're as proud of him as I am. When he was a young man not much older than the two of you, he and thousands like him confronted the German Army, one of the best led and best equipped armies the world has ever known. It was a vicious battle without quarter, and we successfully pushed them out of France back to their homeland and made them surrender unconditionally. All of us were afraid. Your dad did his duty and looked after his men in spite of being frightened. Sometime you should ask him what it took to earn the Combat Infantrymen's Badge and the Silver Star I pinned on his muddy, battle-worn dungaree jacket at the outskirts of Normandy during a brief lull in the fighting."

The self-conscious Ford took a deep breath and said, "Your daughter Cera looks a lot like you, Sir. It has been good to see you again, Colonel. I should tell you that all of us in the outfit were thankful that you were in command. We never really had a chance to say it before, but thanks for all you did for us. We knew that we had the best and would have followed you anywhere any time. I just noticed your cane, Colonel, and I salute you again."

"Thanks, Ford. I appreciate the kind words. It was a different world twenty-five years ago and I'm just as glad as you that our families don't ever have to experience what we went through."

"I believe you're right, Sir. I'll say good-bye for now. See you around."

Cera watched Sergeant Ford make his way across the hall. "The men under your command loved you didn't they, Dad?" Hearing a stranger that knew her father reinforced what Cera and Karen had always known.

"All of them earned my respect and admiration. It was truly a privilege to observe first-hand what the American citizen-soldier is really made of. Well, lets go back upstairs before we go into the conference room. I'm going to bring a raincoat to wear over my uniform. The Channel will be damp and cool. I see that some people are already wearing name tags. We'll probably get them at the reception table."

"I'll go up to get your raincoat, Dad. Wait for me here in the lobby," suggested Cera.

Troy leaned against the wall in the lobby scanning everyone going through. A few men he recognized but could not recall their names without the name tags. He noticed a young infantryman escorting a woman wearing glasses. The second lieutenant made eye contact with him and acknowledged his presence with a nod of his head. Troy stared with stark disbelief at the woman as she was led into the conference room. He felt weak and sought the support of a nearby bench. He must have been seeing things, he could have sworn that the lady that just passed him was Gail!

He continued to stare at the steady line of people passing into the conference room. He cried to himself: "It can't be Gail." She was dead, and her memory was one of the main reasons he came here in the first place. He had planned to look up her grave at the Normandy Cemetery where thousands were buried. He was concerned that he might be losing his mind. It had to be the same woman Cera had spoken about in the restroom.

Cera saw him sitting on a bench near the door with an unsettled look on his face that worried her. The trip was going to be more difficult on him than she anticipated. Maybe it was not such a good idea after all, she mused. His reservoir of strength was already at a very low point. If stress continued to build she was prepared to insist that they leave the tour early.

"I've got your cap and raincoat, Dad. My plastic jacket and hood should be enough for me in case it does rain. You don't look so good. Is anything wrong?"

"No, Cera. I was just thinking about something," Troy answered, unwilling to elaborate or share his thoughts with her. "I'm going to need the name tags to recall a lot of names I have long since forgotten. I remember faces not names. I see that they have a supply at the table near the door. Would you mind getting a couple of them for us, please?"

Cera picked up two of the tags and returned to the bench with her father to write their names on the labels. She placed the adhesive side of the tag against her father's right chest and did the same to hers.

"C'mon, Dad. We want to hear what's being planned."

She offered him her arm to help him stand. He took it and accompanied her into the rear of the conference room where they took seats so that they could see the podium off to their left. The travel agency sponsoring the tour had hired several retired officers to facilitate the logistics and movement of the people to the sites of historical and personal interest.

A speaker took the stand and raised his hands for silence. He spoke in a clear authoritative tone. "Welcome friends and families of friends. On this twenty-fifth anniversary of our momentous assault against fortress Europe, we unite again in common cause to pay tribute to our fallen comrades. Time has not diminished their legacy of courage and valor. We also return to the scene of the most horrific period of our lives when we, as younger men, were called upon to defend the rights of a free people. Each of us has our unique reason for being here. For most of us, it will remain unspoken. This morning we're crossing the English Channel to Normandy on a fast ferry boat capable of accommodating everyone. Buses are now waiting for us at Normandy to tour the battlefields of France. Our first stop will be the Normandy Cemetery which is the resting place of thousands of our brave comrades in arms.

"Hotels and Inns throughout the Normandy region have been reserved for your convenience. I'll discuss the hospitality arrangements in detail later after we arrive in France. Dress warm for the crossing. If anyone needs assistance please let it be known and don't be too proud to ask for it if needed.

"Buses are right outside the hotel. They'll take us to the ferry dockside. I hope this journey back in time is rewarding and fulfilling for all of you. Good luck and God Bless."

Troy and Cera were among the first to leave the room and board one of the waiting buses. Troy scanned the people on the bus to see if the woman he had seen was present. He didn't notice her or the young Lieutenant.

"We can keep our rooms here in England, Cera. I'll want to come back to England before we leave for home if you don't mind," said Troy, watching for Cera's response. She was emotionally and intellectually affected by the solemnity and importance of this trip. He loved her for that. She could be playful and energetic one minute, and pensive and reflective another. Her thoughts and feelings ran deep. In that respect, they were a lot alike.

The bus was full and began its route to the Channel docks on the eastern shore. Troy was emotionally distraught. He looked at Cera and asked her a question, apprehensive about what she might answer.

"Cera. Do you remember that blind lady you met in the restroom?"

"Of course, Daddy. What about it?"

"Did you get her name?"

"Yes, it was a Mrs. Malone."

Chapter Eleven

Blood drained from Troy's face. Cera saw the shock her answer gave to her father and was confused. Things were happening around her that she did not completely understand, and she was concerned. She had seen the fainting spell the blind lady had in the dining room and saw her son carry her out. What was the cause? Why was she so upset in the powder room? Cera thought it was more than simply being disoriented in a strange place. Now the name Malone put her father in a state of near panic. He stared out the window, speechless for the balance of the trip to the dock.

The large ferry boat was receiving passengers and vehicles for the Channel crossing. The bus carrying Troy and Cera was parked in the cavernous interior of the ferry. Most got out of the bus for the one hour trip across the Channel and lined the rails remembering how it had been. Troy needed air and walked up the inclined walkway to the open first deck. He leaned against the railing and breathed deeply. The moist cool, air revived his flagging spirits. Cera accompanied him holding her inquiring tongue and worried in silence. She had never seen him in such a state of shock as he now exhibited.

"Dad, may I get you something to drink? You look pale. Is everything all right with you?"

"I'll be fine, Cera. I'm a little overwhelmed, that's all," he replied absently, continuing to stare at the point of land that had so frightened him and Gail twenty-five years ago.

"I'm going to the concession area for some hot coffee or tea. It's cool here. Would you like some?" Cera asked puzzled by his moodiness.

"I'd like that. I'll take regular black coffee if they have any. If not I'll take tea."

"Stay here at the rail so that I'll know where to find you," Cera told him, kissing him on the cheek.

"I'll be closer to the bow of the ship, Honey. I always liked the feel of a ship plowing its way through the waves."

"I'll be back as soon as I can," promised Cera.

Troy carefully made his way towards the front of the ship. Fewer people were gathered there where the spray sometimes came over the rails. The movement of the ship was much more pronounced at the bow than at midship. The ferry blew its whistle three times before it left the dock. The powerful engines increased in revolutions pulsating through the deck plates as the ship was thrust sideways away from the dock. The unexpected movement caught Troy slightly off balance. He grasped for the railing bumping into a woman leaning against the rail looking across the Channel. He was able to use his cane and the rail to stabilize himself, upset that he was so helpless.

"I'm sorry, Ma'am. I lost my balance," apologized Troy.

The woman tensed when she heard his voice and continued to look toward the water. Troy saw that it was the same person he had seen earlier. The reality started his heart pounding.

"Is that you, Troy?" A voice he could never forget echoed through his memory.

"Gail... It can't be... Is it really you?" He was at a loss for words. She turned to face him. It was Gail! She was clinging to the rail for support much like Troy. Here they were, face to face, twenty-five years after they had said good-bye and promised to meet again. He was puzzled and full of questions.

"This is as much a shock to me as it is to you, Troy. I was wondering if you might be on this tour. I knew that you were because I heard a man calling to you in the dining hall," confessed Gail, filled with conflicting emotions and a desperate desire to get away from him so that she would not have to explain her situation.

"I met you in the hotel lobby yesterday. I knew it was you, yet a person's imagination can do a lot of crazy things after all the years. I thought you were dead, Gail. I looked all over for you, not knowing what had happened. It almost drove me crazy."

"It was a long time ago, Troy. As you can see I've changed."

It was an awkward moment for both of them. Troy saw that she was wearing dark glasses recalling Cera's chance meeting with Gail. She seemed frightened of him and wanted to get away as quickly as possible. Before they could say another word, Gail's son, interrupted them with two paper cups of hot tea.

"Is everything all right, Mother?" he asked, looking at Troy then at his mother with a puzzled look on his face.

"I'm afraid I lost my balance and fell against your mother, Lieutenant," replied Troy, flushed with the discovery and not quite knowing what to do about it.

"I understand, Colonel," said the young lieutenant, holding her hand while she grasped the cup.

Troy had a feeling that his presence was not welcome. "I had better find a bench to sit on. The Channel is rougher than I expected. Nice meeting you Lieutenant and you, too, Mrs. Malone," he said and turned to walk away, bumping into Cera, who was also carrying two cups of tea.

"Father, are you ill? Is something wrong?" she demanded impatiently. She saw Gail and her son, then looked at her father again, more confused and concerned for him than ever. "Come, Dad. You've got to get off your feet. You don't look very well." Without another word, she threw one of the cups overboard and guided Troy into the large sitting area at the center of the ferry.

Alan also escorted his mother to a seating section away from Cera and Troy. She was crying uncontrollably. Alan was worried about her, she never acted this way. He came to the conclusion that her distress was centered somehow around the highly decorated Colonel Hansen, and made a mental note that he and the Colonel had to talk. In the meantime, he made his mother promise to sit quietly at the seating section while he checked out the possibility of locating a place where she could lie down to rest. The ship had a small infirmary. Alan asked for permission to use it if he deemed that his mother's situation justified its use.

The last thing he wanted to do was to question her about something she was reluctant to talk about. They had always been close to each other and had talked freely about everything. Her openness and ability to understand were a part of her generous nature. She had demonstrated her strong will numerous times over the years, and he was proud of her high spirits and courage to take on tasks, such as teaching at a high school, that would have been daunting even for a person capable of seeing well. Within two years after Alan was born, she had completed a course in Braille and became certified to teach at a high school in Amesbury, Massachusetts. She soon became a beloved figure to the students and faculty at that institution.

"What's wrong, Ma?" asked Alan, feeling helpless and not knowing what to do. "I'm beginning to think that this trip was a mistake. Do you think we should cut it short and go home early?"

"No, we're not going to abandon our plans to visit the area where I was wounded," Gail stubbornly responded. She took his hands in hers and held them with a firm grip. "I apologize for putting you through this kind of ordeal, Son. You must be filled with questions."

"I have a few, Mom, that's for sure. I must confess that I don't have a clue as to what is making you so emotional. I know that there's something about this Colonel Hansen guy that pushes you over the edge."

"So he's a Colonel?" mused Gail.

"Yes, and a highly decorated one at that. He's earned the Distinguished Service Cross and several Bronze Stars. Right now he walks with a cane and a pronounced limp. He wears some Vietnam service ribbons. Do you recall that girl that helped you in the restroom?"

"Yes, her name was Cera, a lovely girl."

"Well, she's his daughter."

"I knew that there was something special about her," cried Gail with a sigh.

"If I remember correctly, the other night in the dining hall you fainted instantly after we heard someone call Colonel Hansen's name. It may have been a coincidence but I'm beginning to connect some dots that point to him as the source of your discomfort. Do you want to tell me or is it none of my business?"

"I'm sorry, Alan. I can't tell you anything now. I'm not trying to be secretive or deceptive, it's just that I can't!"

"I can accept that, Ma. I would do anything to protect you and keep you from getting hurt. I've seen you crying and unhappy more on this trip since we arrived in England than at any time in my life. I know that revisiting places where trauma took place can be a frightening, even a painful ordeal. To some it can be a cleansing encounter. I'm a soldier and I understand that."

"I was hoping that I could share with you some of what it was like for me in that terrible war. I was a Navy nurse attached to the Army. I had a vision of you and I returning together to the scene that influenced what the rest of my life would be like. In a way I was selfish to think that it would take place in a vacuum. It can't be isolated from the same desire of others who dreamed the same thing. Thousands have the same memories."

"Ma, did you know this Colonel Hansen during the war? He's about your age."

"Please don't press me for details, Alan," Gail pleaded. "Someday we'll talk about this again. Right now, I just want to continue the tour that we've been planning for years."

"If that's the way you want it Ma, I'll go along with you," answered Alan, determined to speak to Colonel Hansen.

Cera and Troy sat quietly on the bench. People all around them were talking. Cera did not initiate conversation. She passed the tea in her hand to Troy with orders for him to drink it. He took it without saying a word. Cera was mystified over the connection between her father and the blind lady. In a flash, it came to her. Mrs. Malone's name tag had her listed as Mrs. G. Malone, U.S. Navy Nurse attached to the Sixth Medical Battalion, U.S.A. The "G" had to stand for Gail. The mysterious blind lady was the echo from her father's past – the "Gail" he had talked about in his sleep. Now she understood the emotional upheaval taking place within her father and the blind lady. She was anxious to ask for more, but the withdrawn look on his face made her stop.

Troy noticed a triumphant look come over his daughter's face and he assumed that the intuitive child had figured out who Gail was. She seemed content with that knowledge and did not press him for added detail. His discovery of Gail on the tour did nothing but cultivate questions in search of answers. Why didn't she contact him? How come she wasn't on the Army's list of survivors? What ever happened to that solemn pledge they made to meet at a predetermined place one hundred and eighty days after Victory in Europe? Questions clogged his brain. How did she lose her sight? Her Son's presence begged the question where was her husband? So many questions, so few answers...

The ferry landed at a large dock in France. French customs had already checked each person on the ferry as it crossed the Channel, so they drove directly in their respective bus to the hotel reception center near the Normandy Cemetery and Memorial above the bloody Omaha Beaches. Some of the buses were taking small groups of visitors to different locations around the landing beaches.

Cera was anxious to get her father into a bed for a rest. He was an emotional wreck. He did not complain, for he felt exhausted and realized that he had reached his limit. She successfully tucked him into a bed and watched him close his eyes and fall asleep. Cera left a note for him next to his bed that she was in the dining room and would be back shortly.

Troy woke two hours later much refreshed from the rest. He saw the note and left the room in search of the dining room and Cera. In the corridor outside their room he passed Lieutenant Malone, Gail's son. There was a determined look on his face.

"Colonel Hansen, may I have a word with you?"

"Of course, Lieutenant," answered Troy, stopping in the corridor.

"Irrespective of the differences in our military rank I wanted to search you out and speak to you about my mother," Alan stated with a firm set to his jaw.

Troy noticed the seriousness of his intentions and said: "Please feel free to speak your mind, Lieutenant."

"My mother did not want to make this trip to France and England. I insisted because it might allow her to put a lot of ugly memories to rest. Now, I see her on the verge of a breakdown, and I must warn you, senior rank or not, that I will defend her against any and all hurtful alliances. She's paid enough and I won't tolerate anything which increases her anxieties or threatens her well-being. I'm asking you as an officer to another officer, regardless of rank, exactly what your intentions are? So far all of the despair she's had on this trip has been centered around you, Sir."

"My intentions are to continue on the tour as planned, Lieutenant. I have no desire to make your mother unhappy or in any way feel uncomfortable. I have observed how supportive you are of her and admire you for that. I cannot tell you anything more, Lieutenant. You may feel that's an inadequate response and I don't blame you, but if you seek more information you'll have to get it from your mother."

"Well, Sir. I've questioned her and got just about the same answer."

"Give it some time, Lieutenant. These types of reunions are famous for dredging up old memories that have been suppressed. Most of them are painful and long-standing. I can attest to that personally. Don't press your mother too hard and continue to support whatever she asks of you. I am the last person in the world to want to hurt her," Troy confided to the young officer.

"I believe that now, Sir. Perhaps I was jumping to conclusions and apologize for my inappropriate behavior to a superior officer," Alan admitted quickly.

"You don't need to apologize to me, Lieutenant. Like I said, I've seen the way you protect her. She's lucky to have you. I notice that you wear a West Point ring. What year did you graduate?"

"I graduated in the Spring of 1968 and went immediately to Vietnam."

"I notice your Combat Infantrymen's Badge. You earned that early in your career as an Army officer. I've valued mine above all the rest," Troy truthfully told him.

"We're in agreement on that, Sir. Well, I should be getting back to mother. I hope you accept my apology. Good night, Sir."

"Good night, Lieutenant Malone. May I shake your hand?" asked Troy, liking the way the young officer handled himself.

"It's my pleasure, Sir," said Alan, shaking Troy's hand and saluting him. On his way down the corridor, Alan shook his head at the unusual conversation he and Colonel Hansen had just had.

Troy smiled as the young officer walked away. He had that sharp West Point look about him. He found Cera sitting at a large table with several of his old company buddies. They recognized that her name was Hansen and asked if she was Troy's daughter. Once they were introduced to each other it was like one happy family. Troy was relieved to join them. The years had aged them, but it had not dampened that same spirit that held them together throughout the war. Cera thought her dad looked better. The men liked him and she enjoyed watching him get wrapped up in old Army stories with his buddies, thankful that the Gail business had been placed on hold for the evening.

Chapter Twelve

Time had dimmed many of the names for Troy, but enough facial and body characteristics remained from younger days that recognition was possible. The name tags helped and saved a lot of embarrassing encounters. Most people began their conversation with the words, "Do you remember?"

Troy was especially glad to see one of his former platoon leaders, Lieutenant James Calvin, a short stocky man with bushy eyebrows. He was a corn farmer from Iowa.

"Jim Calvin," cried Troy, approaching the table. "I'd recognize you anywhere. It's nice to see you again."

"Captain Hansen," replied Jim, getting out of his chair to hug his former company commander. "Age has been kind to you, Troy. Your lovely daughter was just telling us about your wounds. Sit down. Man it's great to see you."

Troy took a seat beside Cera and acknowledged the others sitting around the table, a platoon sergeant and two corporals along with their wives. They looked familiar, but he could not recall their names. Cera introduced them and suddenly Troy was taken back to the war years. Twenty-five years ago they had been young soldiers fresh out of high school. The war experience had turned them into mature adults in a short period of time.

Those who sat at the table had been part of the infantry company that he trained and ordered into battle. Not once did the young soldiers ever falter, no matter how difficult the fighting. Troy carried the memories of every man close to his heart. His company and hundreds of others just like it were hurled at the formidable Fortress Europe. At Normandy they cracked the outer shell of defenses with a level of courage and valor that was maintained until the Germans surrender unconditionally almost a year later. Men capable of accomplishing that were capable of accomplishing anything. They had earned Troy's respect and the admiration of the western world. His buddies at the table were representative of that very special generation. Once the enemy had been beaten, they took off their uniforms and began the mighty task of embracing the future with a fervor equal to their valor on the battlefield.

"What are you doing in civilian life, Jim?" asked Troy.

"I've taken over the family farm raising corn and soy beans. Sue and I have four kids. One of them is in Vietnam now. We worry a lot about him..."

"It's a hard place to fight," said Troy. "I think that the Germans fought smarter than the North Vietnamese. I was glad to get away from the stinking jungle. My leg wound probably put the finishing touches on my Army career, but I'm prepared for civilian status."

Meeting old acquaintances and friends was an uplifting experience, yet there was a serious, nervous undertone of unspoken apprehension. They all had much in common, but the experience of combat and the way it had been handled over the years was very much an individual and a private matter. Jim Calvin was the first to talk about the reason they returned to Normandy.

"Omaha Beach was my baptism to combat and an introduction to what it was like to command young soldiers on the battlefield. It wasn't anything like they lectured to us at Officer Candidate School at Benning. I remember one kid, a skinny boy from Tennessee with a slow moderate southern drawl. I can't remember his name but we jumped off the landing craft ramp into a couple of feet of water. He had the bad luck of stepping into a deep hole and went out of sight sinking like a rock. He had managed to splash his way up to get a breath of air. Then two of his buddies yanked him to shallower water. He was so slow in talking that he did not have time to yell for help before going under. He floundered several times and never uttered a word. We were pretty well loaded with ammo and gear, as you may recall."

Jim had a painful look on his face remembering what it was like. His wife put her protective arm around him.

"That's all right, Jim," Troy said, trying to console him. "You did a great job of getting your platoon off the beach."

"That boy from Tennessee was my first casualty..." Jim continued in a strained voice. The memories were vivid and immediate. "He shook the excess water off him and was checking his M-1 when a mortar round or a rifle grenade, I never knew which, cut him in two. His blood splattered all over me. In that fraction of a second when the explosion took place, he looked at me with those big brown eyes he had. They were filled with terror. He uttered two words, 'Oh – No!' a split second before dying. I can still hear them in my dreams. He was only seventeen."

A waiter came to their table to take their orders. Troy was not hungry. The mood at the table was somber and reflective. Every veteran had similar tales in the dark recesses of their memory. Battlefield tours are rarely celebrations, they're more appropriately called pilgrimages. Veterans, such as those that sat at the table with Troy and Cera, sometimes found it difficult to share their experiences. Many were simply too painful and grotesque to describe. The image and feelings remained isolated in their souls until memories triggered by associated thoughts or events brought them to the surface. That phenomenon was now taking place. Sharing the experience with loved ones was an important step in dealing with them.

The next day, Troy and Cera took a bus to the Normandy Cemetery and Memorial located on a bluff overlooking the Omaha Beaches. Over nine thousand American warriors are buried on the perfectly manicured battlefield. It was a warm sunny day with soft cumulous clouds floating in the blue skies above the crosses and Stars of David laid out in parade ground precision.

Troy could remember when he buried a few men in a makeshift grave not far from the coast. They were his first losses as a company commander. Writing the letters to families back home that their beloved son or husband was killed in action, was a difficult thing to do. He was never able to compose a letter to a grieving mother and make it easier for her to accept the tragedy. No matter what was written after the announcement of death, it was passed over and forgotten. The youth and innocence of the fallen soldiers still bothered him. The average age of the men in his company that were lost in the Normandy Campaign was eighteen years. The first burial was composed of forty men.

The cemetery was beautifully maintained. A soft breeze blew from the Channel to the plateau overlooking the landing sites. Twenty-five years after the invasion it was possible to find peace within the cemetery. It was in stark contrast to the devastation and chaos of the battlefield. Instead of turmoil and anguish, many found a deep sense of serenity and appreciation for the sacrifice of so many. It was sacred ground where the spirits of youthful warriors could be felt by those who took the time to listen to the heartbeat of the earth.

Troy and Cera came away from the cemetery with a renewed respect and admiration for what thousands had given up for them. The experience questioned their worthiness of such noble sacrifices. They turned to look back at the endless rows of crosses. A cloudy mist filled Troy's eyes. "France damned well better respect what these young men did here!" Cera saw him slowly shake his head at the magnitude of the cost in American lives.

"I hope they are worthy, Dad. But I would not be surprised that in a few more years the sacrifice will be forgotten or denied," declared Cera, placing an arm around him and holding him tight. "Seeing all of those graves make me more appreciative than ever of having you survive the horrific campaign."

In the meantime, Gail and Alan had hired a private taxi to take them to the location where she was wounded by German artillery. Alan had researched the incident while he was at West Point and knew precisely where the medical battalion Gail was attached to had established its tents and supply depot. It had been an initial surgical treatment center for the more seriously injured soldiers. It was an elaborate facility with state of the art equipment available for the wounded within minutes from the battlefields.

Those who took the gamble of placing it so close to the active lines believed that the Germans would honor the facility. Consequently, it was profusely decorated with Red Cross insignias. German artillery batteries ignored the flags or did not know they were there. The complex was the recipient of a heavy bombardment wiping out most of the battalion members and countless numbers of wounded soldiers. It was the heaviest loss suffered by the Army's Medical Corps during the European campaign.

The location was west of the town of Caen which had already been partially liberated by paratroopers when the battalion set up their tents. Gail was part of a brigade of Naval Nurses that had volunteered to help their Army brethren while their hospital ship underwent repairs in England.

The taxi drove through the fertile agricultural region of France famous for wines and sugar beets. The driver spoke some English and promised to show Alan some examples of the hedgerows that surrounded farmer's fields. They began at the edge of the coastal plain and extended inland for miles. The Citroen pulled into a level field newly plowed and seeded to sugar beets. It was about ten acres in size with access openings at the opposite side of the field. No fences were needed. Surrounding the fields were strips of thick growths of small trees and shrubs four to ten feet in width. It was impossible for a person to get through them without cutting some of the vegetation.

Alan described the hedgerows to his mother adding how the Germans had positioned machine guns so that they had overlapping fields of fire. Once he had observed several fields similarly constructed, he shook his head and marveled at the advantage the Germans, with a minimum number of men, held over the Americans.

"I don't see how we got through them," explained Alan.

"Our losses were severe at that time in the campaign," recalled Gail. "The hedgerow region consumed more men than the heavily fortified coastal invasion site. I remember how busy we were with casualties."

"Driver, you may continue towards Caen now," instructed Alan.

"Oui, yes, Sir."

"What did you think about the French countryside, Ma?"

"There wasn't any time to admire the scenery. When we were not busy caring for the wounded we were packing equipment in trucks to be moved forward. We moved several times in three days. My main recollection was that it was impossible to get away from the sounds of gunfire, either enemy or friendly. We also spent a lot of time in foxholes holding our arms over our heads. I was always frightened then. There seemed to be no end to the killing and maiming of young men's bodies."

Alan squeezed her hand. "If you had told me that you were not afraid, I would not have believed you, Ma. I was afraid in Vietnam. There's a lot to be said about fear in combat. It puts you on a high level of alert and helps you maintain a degree of awareness that saves lives."

"I guess it's a human trait we all possess," said Gail, touching the ribbons he had on his chest. "I was hoping that you would never have to experience combat. I was worried all the time you were over there, Alan."

"I'm sure you did, but I've had the best training in the world and I'm proud to be a professional soldier. Thanks to your hard work it became a possibility."

"We're nearing the location of the battalion's campsite," said Gail. "I can feel it."

"You're right, Ma. The train station you had mentioned is on our right and a small pond is on the left. The tracks go over a small concrete bridge at the outlet of the pond. Your site must have been over the roadway bridge and immediately to the right. It's now a large field filled with grape arbors. According to the sign beside the road there's a winery close by."

The driver stopped the Citroen. "This is the location you described to me, Mrs. Malone."

"Thank you driver." Gail opened the door and got out of the automobile. She lifted her chin and faced the east where the German artillery batteries were located. "We all heard the bombardment and made provisions for a rapid flight from the area. I had already been relieved of duty and was waiting for a ride to the Channel when the rolling barrage kept getting closer and closer. The smell of cordite and smoke filled the air. An American artillery battery on the far side of the pond began firing at the Germans as rapidly as they fired at us."

"Where were you in the complex when it began?" asked Alan, realizing how difficult the memories must have been for her.

"There was no time to avoid the barrage. Everyone began to help the wounded into foxholes prepared at several locations. I was helping to carry a stretcher with a seriously wounded young man with curly hair. He had a gaping hole through his lungs. I can still hear the sucking sounds he made breathing. We were afraid, terrorized would be a more fitting description. I can remember hearing a loud noise like a freight train going very fast just before I was lifted off the ground and dropped beside the foxhole. It's strange but I never heard the explosion. You know what happened after that."

"The records indicate that it was the greatest loss of medical members of the war. Did any of your Navy nurse friends survive the blast?"

"A few did because they were relieved several hours before I was. They were already at the coast waiting shipping back to England. The rest were lost along with the Army personnel under the category 'Killed in Action, identity unknown'. I still pray for them."

"It's such a peaceful place now. It's hard to imagine it being the scene of such carnage and death. You're lucky to be alive, Ma. We have that to be thankful for."

"To those who do not know, it may appear to be peaceful but it's filled with the spirits of young men and women who had dreams and aspirations for the future. Imagine the contribution that could have been made to society if the doctors, nurses, and medics had survived the war and gone home to care for those in need. That loss must also be mourned. Whenever I start to feel sorry for my condition I have but to think of those killed here and I'm instantly comforted that I was spared the same fate."

"So am I, Ma. So am I," said Alan, helping her back into the taxi. "As soon as we head back towards Normandy I have a surprise for you."

"A good surprise or a bad surprise?" She was petrified that he was going back to Vietnam as soon as they got back from the tour.

"A good one, Ma," he said placing an arm, around her and kissing her on the forehead. "You're a real trooper. I wish I had half the spunk and determination you have."

"When you really need it, you'll find it within you, Son. I'm glad you could come to France with me. I feel better now."

"When we left home to make this pilgrimage, I had received something I wanted to share with you. Now is as good a time as any," Alan announced, smiling at his mother. "I've just been promoted to first lieutenant and the next time I have a chance to get to a PX I plan to purchase my silver bars."

"I knew it could not be long. You deserve it, Son. They'll look good on you even if I can't see them." exclaimed Gail.

She was completely at ease in his presence. Over the years, they had shared a close relationship. She was a very independent woman and appreciated the way Alan measured his protection, allowing her to do all that she could on her own within the bounds of safety. She loved him for that.

Gail was reminded of another time in her life when she had shared a promotion with a soldier. She never forgot that day she had pinned captain bars on Troy's uniform. A similar pride filled her heart for Alan. A warm smile came over her face. She searched in her purse and clutched two silver First Lieutenant Bars in her hand. She had kept them as a souvenir from Troy. It was the single tangible thing she possessed from that period of her life.

"Alan I have something for you," she said holding the two bars in her open palm. "Over the years they've been a reminder of that part of my life. May I pin them on your uniform?"

"I've seen them off and on over the years," Alan replied. "You occasionally wear them on your blazer lapel or on your hat. Were they from your Navy Nurse uniform?"

"No. I was only an ensign with a gold bar," answered Gail. "I can tell you that they once belonged to a very brave soldier that I knew many years ago."

Alan turned so that his mother could replace the bars. She was tense and her hands shook as she completed the job and kissed him on the cheek.

"Thanks, Ma. This promotion probably means that I'll be assigned to a battalion as exec officer. I'll try to live up to the standards of the soldier who previously wore them. Is there anything else you want to tell me?"

"Just that I love you, and am so proud of you..."

Chapter Thirteen

Cera and Troy took one of the private taxicabs made available to the tour members, asking the driver to head inland toward Falaise. It had been at the western outskirts of the town that his company of infantry was able to break away from the costly hedgerows and move towards Paris. Some soldiers had fond memories of the French people when they were liberated from the oppressive Germans. Troy's experience was less than complimentary. He remembered how a large portion of the French population terrorized the Jewish elements of their country, frequently being more brutal to the Jews than the Germans. He had always thought of the French allies as being weak and untrustworthy.

He told Cera how his company had surrounded a large farm where sugar beets, potatoes, and corn were grown. Two French families had lived there. They were allowed to continue with their agricultural pursuits. War or no war, everyone needed food. Three of the workers on the farm had some Jewish blood in their veins, and the family that owned the farm had sheltered them from the German Gestapo and the French Police, which were often more vicious when dealing with the Jews. Local Frenchmen had betrayed the farm owners and the complex was raided by the French Police who came looking for the Jews they knew were somewhere on the property.

They began shooting the farmer's family one at a time shouting in loud voices that those who knew of the Jew's presence were responsible for the killing. Three adults were shot by the senior policeman, a local man known to be a Nazi sympathizer. After the third man was shot, the Jews turned themselves in to save the lives of those who had befriended them. They in turn were shot in cold blood by the trigger happy policeman. They left leaving six bleeding bodies in the farmyard.

The above incident had taken place just days before Troy's company surrounded and secured the farm complex. That night he heard of the murders. The most senior member of the farm family was still traumatized by what had happened. He begged Troy to send soldiers into the town so that he could point out the police official who had perpetrated the murderous outrage. Troy was not sure if the town was liberated yet, but agreed to lead a patrol composed of two Jeeps and a half-track. The elder gentleman rode in the back seat of the lead Jeep with Troy. As they approached the outskirts of the village a police van almost ran into Troy's Jeep. The elder man became excited and pointed to the officer in the passenger seat of the van as the man responsible for the murders.

Troy ordered his men to surround the van. Four French policemen approached the American soldiers all smiles and full of contrition, pleased that the Americans had pushed the Germans out of the town. Troy ordered the two policemen searched and disarmed, then marched them towards the half-track. The elder farmer leaped from the Jeep and confronted the police officer who had murdered six people including two of his grandsons.

The policeman was a small man, compact and erect, with a clipped mustache. He wore a sneering smirk on his face, except for when the elder approached him and spit in his face. The man recognized the elder and became mortally frightened. Troy did not understand all that was said, but, in that instant, he knew that the elder farmer had been telling the truth. Suddenly, a motorcycle courier rode into the village and passed a message from battalion headquarters to Troy. He was ordered to immediately draw additional ammo and supplies from a supply convoy directly to his rear and continue the advance through the village without delay.

In the meantime, the square was filling with people cheering the liberating Americans.

"What did you do then, Dad?" asked Cera, mesmerized by the recollections of her father.

"My orders had to be carried out as requested, so I promised to return the elder to his farmhouse. My men rounded up the four policemen and turned them over to the townspeople," explained Troy.

"What happened then?"

"I learned later that the crowd allowed two of the policeman to return to their homes. The other two, including the murderous perpetrator, were involved in numerous outrages against the civilian population. The angry crowd clubbed the two policeman to death. It was a just punishment in my view."

"Did you think something like that might happen?" asked Cera shuddering at the decision her father had to make.

"At the time I was driving away, I had a feeling that justice would be better served by those who were victimized by the murders than they would have been if I had turned them into a prisoner of war compound. I can honestly tell you that I had an urge to kill that man myself. He was not a human being, he was a fanatical mad dog deserving any fate they handed out to him," recalled Troy.

"I can understand why you thought that way," confided Cera.

"I was afraid that one of my men would do it for me and we'd be blamed for the atrocity. They all told me afterwards that I did the right thing. The farmer knew what the crowd would do and he was satisfied that justice would be served."

By the time Troy and Cera returned to the hotel it was dark. He unexpectedly announced to Cera that he was prepared to cut the tour short. He saw little advantage in continuing for the next ten days. That evening there was a gala celebration in the large banquet room of the hotel. They planned to attend and to say good-bye to those who were staying for the duration of the tour.

In the meantime, Troy escorted Cera into the dining room, they were both famished. They recognized Alan and Gail at a table across the room. Cera returned Alan's smile.

"There's something about the Lieutenant that makes me feel that I should know him. I can't put my finger on it," said

Cera, watching Troy look at Gail. "She's an attractive lady isn't she?"

"That she is," Troy answered without thinking. "I can read your mind Cera, and we're not going to go there. When the time is right I promise to tell you, but not right now."

"You're just adding to the intrigue, Daddy. Okay, we won't go there as you say. It looks as if the banquet room is filling up. I can hear a lot of the war era songs being played by the band."

"Back then two types of songs were popular. The crazy ones that made you forget the war and maybe smile a little, and the slow songs of home, love, and the sadness and heartache of the times. The latter were by far the more popular. Relationships were relative and frequently of a short duration."

Cera memorized the last sentence. It was a statement of longing and sadness. To her it was significant. Her father looked away from Gail and, self-consciously, stirred his coffee. They ate in silence listening to the music as it wafted through the dining room.

"Shall we go into the room, Dad?" asked Cera finishing her meal.

"Sure if you want," he complied. Seeing Gail nearby and not being able to be with her was unraveling his composure. Something had gone wrong, and he was shattered by the feeling of impotence and insignificance.

The seven piece orchestra was playing a medley of songs germane to the period: *White Cliffs of Dover, That Old Black Magic, Paper Doll* and *I'll Be Seeing You In All The Old Familiar Places*. The latter song, as sung by Vera Lynn, was one of the most popular of all.

Cera and Troy took a seat at a table against a wall and listened to the music. It had poignancy and special meaning to the veterans in the room. Shortly Gail and Alan took seats at a table on the same side of the room. Gail seemed to be uncomfortable in a room where she could be seen, yet could not see anyone else. A set of slow waltzes began and the dance floor started to fill with couples.

Troy could not keep his eyes from Gail. Alan had asked her something and she shook her head. A second later, Alan

110

approached Cera and Troy's table. "Good evening, Colonel, and Miss Hansen. May I have this dance?"

"That would be nice, Lieutenant," replied Cera, slipping into his arms.

Gail was sitting alone. Troy left his table and took a seat next to her.

"Hello, Gail. It's me, Troy."

"I could tell by your after shave lotion. You still use the same brand," she recalled.

"I do. Cera and Alan are dancing together. I was never much of a dancer. Would you like to take a chance with me? I believe I can do it leaving my cane behind if I can balance on you."

A sudden shiver crossed her face. "I'm blind Troy!" she said in denial.

"So what! I'll try to do the leading."

"Do you promise to bring me back to the chair if it doesn't work?" she asked hesitantly.

"I promise, Gail. I have no desire to make you feel uncomfortable," he said, placing her hand on his arm. "The last time we did this was mid-May, 1944 at a canteen in England."

"That was a long time ago, Troy. The world has turned over many times since then."

Troy took her in his arms and slowly began to pick the 1-2-3 beat of the waltz, holding her tight in his arms. She held him close. Her touch electrified his body. The top of her head came to his chin. He was holding his Gail in his arms! It was almost unbelievable.

"How have you been since the war, Gail?"

"I've been busy and preoccupied trying to build a new life. I don't complain. I beg you Troy, please don't ask all those questions you have in your heart," she pleaded in a low voice.

"If you insist," he whispered in her ear. "Let me say that I never forgot you even after I was married and my two daughters Cera and Karen were born. Memories of you have haunted me for half of my life. I never stopped loving you Gail, never…"

She laid her head against his chest. He felt like crushing her. She began to cry softly. He felt the tenseness in her body.

"I would have climbed any mountain for you Gail, no matter how high. I still would. You have but to ask me."

"Stop, Troy," she pleaded. "We're not the same people and too much time has passed. Let us remember it as the beautiful part of our lives that it was. Now please let it go. We had our time and it was taken away from us. I remember too..."

"It was cruel to let you go when I last saw you beneath the dim street lamp twenty-six years ago. It will be equally difficult to walk away and forget that I've held you in my arms when I've had nightmares believing you to be dead," confessed Troy.

The music stopped. Troy offered his arm and escorted her back to the table.

"It has been special hearing you talk and meeting you again, Troy. Before Alan returns, let me say that you are not the only one to have warm memories, but we cannot resurrect them. Things are different and you must not ask me why. I cannot answer the question. Please don't hate me, Troy."

"Are you that sure, Gail?"

"Yes, it's for the best. I hear Alan and Cera coming towards us. Please, don't be sad, Troy. I ..."

"Hello, Mrs. Malone and Dad," said Cera in a happy mood. "You two did pretty good out there on the floor for a man using a cane."

"Hello again, Cera," replied Gail, holding her hand. "Your father does better on the floor than he lets on."

"Dancing with Cera was like dancing with a butterfly, light and easy," injected Alan. "It's nice to see you again, Colonel."

"I see that you've been promoted Lieutenant, congratulations."

"Cera was telling me about Warrant Officer John Lamprey. He flew my platoon on several missions. He's one cool helicopter pilot. Once he inserted us in an area with a heavy fire-fight underway and never hesitated to place his machine between the enemy and the troops exiting it. He also pulled me and a squad out of a really tight spot under withering machine gun fire. We owe our lives to him. You wish him well for me the next time you see him."

"I'll be glad to, Alan. John seems to be that strong silent type that has served our country so well over the years," Troy answered.

"If you'll excuse me," announced Gail. "I believe I'll retire. It's been a long difficult day. Goodnight, Cera, and you too, Troy."

"Good night, Gail," said Troy.

"Did Dad tell you that we were planning to return home tomorrow?" mentioned Cera.

"No," answered Gail sounding disappointed. "In that case, it has been nice meeting both of you, goodnight."

Cera kissed her on the cheek: "Good night, Mrs. Malone."

"Bless you child," said Gail, hugging her.

"I wish you well, Gail," answered Troy soberly.

"Good-bye, Troy. Thanks for the memories." she reached out and embraced him warmly. "It was nice…"

Troy was rattled from head to his toes. He did not know whether to take her by the shoulders and shake her or turn around and run away. She was not the same person he once knew and he ached to find out what went wrong. She was distant and evasive instead of warm and caring. Cera saw the hesitation on his part and casually tugged on his arm.

"We should be going too, Dad," she insisted. They left the hall in a hurry with Cera on his arm.

"That was an awkward moment, Ma," Alan exclaimed, watching his mother for some reaction. He was upset with her. She had been rude to the colonel. When he had a chance to speak to her she remained distantly proper and a little rude. "What did the colonel do to make you angry? The air was so heavy you could have cut it with a knife. Cera felt it, too, and nudged the Colonel away as quickly as possible. What's going on, Mother?"

"Nothing."

"So far this trip has been a disaster and I'm powerless to know how to help you or comprehend if you want help or not. You tell me nothing, but I know that you're keeping something from all of us and it's torturing you. I love you, Mother, but I think you're using the wrong strategy. To put it another way, bumping into Colonel Hansen has triggered an emotional crisis with you. I just don't understand it."

"You've said that already, Alan," Gail replied sharply.

"I know, but it bears repeating, Ma."

"I was not as rude to Troy as you're trying to imply," she cried in defense of her actions. "For your information I'm not angry at him or at anything he's done. I'm angry at myself."

"Well, I've seen people register emotions before and the colonel just left here as if he was delivered the most hurtful blow in his life. He was dejected and disappointed. If he's not your enemy I'd hate to see the way your friends react to you." remarked Alan, forcefully pushing the limits of his criticism.

She turned away from him and began to cry. "Please take me to my room."

"Of course Ma. I'm sorry. I apologize."

"No you're correct. It's me. I'm angry at decisions and choices I've made over the years. Troy was nothing but a gentle and true friend, and I ended up hurting him because of my mistakes. He's suffered the consequences as much as I have and he's blameless. That's what I'm angry about, Son."

Alan escorted her to their rooms and helped her remove the blazer and small hat she wore, crying harder than ever. She laid on the bed and turned away from Alan. It was her way of saying leave me alone. He kissed her on the cheek.

"Is there anything I can do, Ma?" She shook her head the way he knew she would. She had a tendency to fight her battles alone without interference. "If you need me, I'll be in the sitting room."

Alan dropped onto the couch and lit a cigarette, breathing deeply before exhaling the smoke. Normally he didn't smoke much because cigarettes ended up burning small holes in his uniforms and it became too expensive to replace them. It was impossible to understand just what forces were at work on his mother. He felt sorry for the colonel and Cera who were quick to pick up on the brush-off his mother had given them. Cera was an alert and intelligent girl and he liked her. She was fun to be with. He also liked the Colonel. There was a strong sense of character and integrity to the soldier and Alan liked his modest style.

Two floors up in the same hotel, Troy was troubled by Gail's dismissal. He had held her hand and knew that she wore a wedding ring. Where was her husband? He shrugged his shoulder thinking that she could say the same thing about him. He was most struck by what Gail refused to talk about. She intentionally ignored the agreed meeting place after the war as if it was insignificant, and dismissed the fact that he had determined to the best of his ability that she must have been dead. Her failure to inform him of that hurt the most. Why did she keep her survival away from him? Her silence was the most hurtful tool at her disposal. It wasn't fair. It just wasn't fair...

Chapter Fourteen

The next morning Cera and Troy took the first available boat back to England. She was an avid souvenir collector and before they left France she purchased a couple of local French papers which had covered the reunion celebrations. She also picked up a packet of pictures taken at various locations and groups of people on the tour. She shoved them into her suitcase and ran to a cab waiting to take them to the boarding docks. Troy had a defeated look on his face. He was silent and morose.

"C'mon, Dad. There's nothing here for us. Whatever it was that you hoped to find on this trip you must evaluate for yourself. I hope you can find some consolation and peace of mind. As for me, it has been important. It gave me another perspective into the warrior psyche that you have been most of your adult life. For that, the trip has been rewarding. My appreciation for the price paid for our freedom has increased many times."

"You're a perceptive child, Cera. Surely this trip has turned out differently than expected. Perhaps I held some memories for too long a time. I'm not sure right now. Thanks for coming with me. You've made me proud. I'm ready to go home to the Lake of Three Sorrows where I can think things out and drop a fish line in the water. I wonder if Ashley realizes what a salvation that place is going to be for me."

"I'm sure that's one of the reasons she made it available to you, Dad. I wish she was still around. I miss her a lot," said Cera. "Europe has little appeal to me. I'm ready to go home, too."

They left England on a flight directly to Portland, Maine where their Wagoneer was parked. Troy was quiet and distant for most of the trip. He was returning a different man, bitter and disappointed that his memories conflicted with reality. For twenty-five years he had treasured the memories of him and Gail together. Somewhere in that time span he had elevated them to a significance that she did not share. From the time the plane took off from Heathrow Airport in London Troy had the feeling that he was at the threshold of a new chapter in his life. He and Gail really had little in common now. It was a bitter fact to swallow.

Cera tried to cheer him up on the ride home from Portland. "You know Dad, I'm going to have a hard time giving this rig up when I start school in September."

Troy looked at her and smiled. "Maybe we can work something out for you to drive back and forth for weekends and holidays," he answered with a winsome look. "You can use a smaller less expensive car than this during your college stay. Sorry!"

"I tried anyway," said Cera, pleased that he was able to respond in a playful way. "Do you want to go to Togus first?"

"Yes, they can give me a quick check up and then we can head for home. That's the first time I've referred it to it as 'home'. It has a nice ring to it doesn't it?"

"It does, considering how badly you need the healing powers it's capable of unleashing. Can you put Gail behind you Dad?"

"I don't know, Cera. I'll try, knowing that I should bring that period of my life to an end. I promise, I'll try. Sometime I'll explain it to you in more detail. When it took place it seemed important. Now, twenty-five years later, it has become insignificant. Time heals, and I'm willing to give it a chance to work."

Troy went directly to the out-patient clinic at Togus. Cera excused herself and went to the main desk at the entrance to see if John Lamprey had been admitted yet. She was told that he was in a ward on the top floor. The nurse on duty told her that it was getting late, visiting hours were almost over: "Go ahead, Miss Hansen. He's our celebrity patient and we can make an exception for you. He had visitors earlier that got him upset when they left. Maybe you can cheer him up."

"Thanks, I'll try," Cera answered.

"He's a nice young man. We're proud to have a Maine man wear the Medal of Honor," the nurse explained.

Cera walked in on John as he was buttoning up his hospital johnny. He was having trouble with it and seemed irritated.

"Hello, Warrant Officer Lamprey," Cera announced.

John looked up into her smiling face and grinned. "I was hoping that you'd stop by."

"Dad is at the out-patient clinic for his leg. I took a chance to see if you'd been admitted. It's nice to see you again."

"Why is it that you always bring a ray of sunshine when you visit me? I was shipped to the Walter Reed Hospital in Washington the day I wrote you my last letter. The next day I met the President. He placed the Medal of Honor around my neck. It was a special day. Mom came with me to the Oval Office."

"I'm sure she was proud to see her son awarded our nation's highest honor for bravery," said Cera, pulling a chair next to his bed. John sat up straight in his bed so as to not let his empty sleeve dangle conspicuously. It still made him uncomfortable.

"She was quite emotional," replied John modestly.

"Has your father been to see you, John?" asked Cera wondering why he spoke only of his mother.

"I never knew my father. He was killed during the Battle of the Bulge at Bastogne. I'm what my Mom calls a furlough baby."

"I'm sorry I asked," she said, realizing how the war reached out and touched so many lives in a very cruel way. "I just got back from Normandy. The veterans that I met were remarkable people. That generation did impossible things in a short period of time and asked for nothing except the chance to return home and get on with their lives. I admire them. They had character and courage."

"You've given the issue some thought haven't you?"

"You bet. It's easy when you're an Army brat like me," she smiled.

"How did your father take the reunion? I've heard they can be brutal to those who've denied their experiences for a long period of time," asked John.

"He did better than I expected," answered Cera. "He'll have a few bad nights as a result of the trip. In general I believe that the reunion and the related memories it generated are going to be a positive entity in his handling of ugly war experiences."

"Here comes your father now," announced John, straightening out his hospital robe.

"Hello, Lamprey," Troy greeted him warmly. "How's our newest Medal Of Honor recipient doing? I always knew that Maine raised strong men. You've proven it once again."

"Hi, Colonel. I'm glad you stopped by. Cera has been telling me about your tour of Normandy."

"It went better than anticipated. I was surprised how kind old Father Time has been to some of the men. I was the one with the whitest hair of the group."

"It's becoming to you, Father," exclaimed Cera with a whimsical smile.

"Flattery will get you most anything, young lady," he laughed.

They visited with John Lamprey for an hour. Their conversations covered subjects from the weather to the status of the economy in the State of Maine. Cera and Troy pestered him with questions about how the President was on a person to person basis. John told them that President Nixon was a very warm person genuinely concerned for him and his mother.

"You've been asking a lot of questions about me, what about you, Colonel? What kind of a status report did the doctors give you? You seem to be getting around very nicely with the cane," John asked.

"I'm healing as well as expected according to the doctors. It seems slow to me. I guess I need more time before they can be certain of my ultimate status. I'm returning home with Cera where she can take care of me for the rest of the summer. She's really a pretty good cook. I think she's missing her calling by studying journalism."

"Father, I can't believe you made such an outrageous statement," Cera declared, shaking her head. They all laughed.

"Well, Cera I think we should be heading North." Troy was feeling weary from the long day of traveling. "You're looking well, John. Good luck. I'm proud to salute you. We'll stop by the next time we come to Togus."

"Good-bye, Sir. Thanks for visiting a while."

Troy left the room so that they could say good-bye in private.

"I'm pleased to see that you're making such good progress, John. If you don't mind, I'll continue to write once in a while and as dad said, I'll see you when he comes back for check-ups. You take care now," said Cera.

"Thanks for coming. I've been hoping that you would. So long until next time."

"Until next time, John," said Cera, leaning over to kiss him on the cheek. She left the ward pausing at the door to wave one last time to him.

Troy fell in beside her in the corridor and they walked together to the Wagoneer. She was quiet for a long time and he honored her desire to be alone with her thoughts. He thought he saw something happening between her and the brave young helicopter pilot. He knew how intense and overpowering feelings of the heart can be. Time does not diminish their ability to dominate and influence every facet of life. She drove the Wagoneer with precision and skill making good time. Troy laid his head against the back of the seat and fell asleep. He woke up as Cera turned off the ignition key.

"I'm sorry I slept all that time, Cera."

"I didn't mind. You snored a lot. That means you're exhausted. If I'm going to take care of you, you'd better listen to me and not disobey orders."

"Aye Aye, Sir," he answered with mock respect. "Now that I've had a nap, I probably won't be able to sleep. You know what?"

"Not unless you tell me," Cera replied flippantly.

"Remind me to give you my lecture on respecting your elders. I was intending to tell you that I was hungry when you interrupted my line of thinking," Troy exclaimed, grinning at his daughter. They had always enjoyed good-natured banter.

"So am I, Dad."

"We haven't been doing much grocery shopping since Ashley left have we?"

"She left the place pretty well stocked," said Cera. "How about some coffee with a peanut butter and jelly sandwich?"

"That appeals to me. I've been a peanut butter addict for a long time. I'll make the coffee, you can make the sandwiches. I flattered you a little bit in front of John you know. It's true that you do a pretty tolerable job and I appreciate the effort, but your coffee is weak stuff. As a matter of fact, it hardly qualifies as coffee. Troubled water is a more fitting description. You watch your old dad count out the scoops of coffee. That's plural, not singular..."

"Okay, know-it-all, I stand corrected and will let you do it from now on." She put her arms around him and continued: "Remind me to tell my Dad that I love him very much."

"I will every day."

They ate their midnight snack in relative silence. Cera was beginning to see the father she remembered. Normally he was full of fun and at times could be a maddening tease. Home was beginning to work its magic on him. He had rarely joked around with Beth but with Karen and Cera, he frequently made irreverent comments that kept them alert and on guard.

That night Cera laid in her bed in the loft listening to the call of the loons across the lake feeling cozy and secure in the tiny alcove. She thought of John Lamprey. Things seemed to feel right when she was with him. She believed it to be mutual. Most of her young adult life she had made friends easily and went out on dates with different young men. Her out-going personality cultivated friendships, but none had ever made her feel like she did towards John. She had often wondered how it would feel to have someone in her life that was truly special. John had earned that title with his courage and inherent decency. First, he had won her admiration and respect. Now, perhaps, he had won her heart! It was a new experience for her.

Before surrendering to sleep, Cera could not get the reunion out of her mind. There was something about it that bothered her. Gail and her son, Alan, had dominated her thoughts since they left France. Cera climbed down the ladder from the loft and began rummaging through her bags stored in the extra bedroom that Ashley had used. She turned on the light and checked the newspaper photos and news stories of the tour.

On one of the photos Alan and Gail were prominently shown in the conference meeting room. Several of the pictures in the souvenir packets she purchased also contained pictures of Alan and Gail. She laid them out on the bed and took an old photo of her father from World War Two, placing it beside the new photos.

The resemblance between the two soldiers was remarkable!

Chapter Fifteen

It was an enchanting evening. The earth was hushed in the solitude of the night. Troy sat on the swinging couch on the porch and watched the last rays of the sun fall behind the granite mass known as Squaw Mountain. Shortly after, the distinctive call of the whippoorwills echoed across the water. The calls came almost every evening at nine o'clock. He had tried to locate the melancholic sounding birds with a pair of Army night binoculars, but was unsuccessful in getting a glimpse of the illusive birds. In between the whippoorwills and the call of the loons the evening was silent enough that he could hear his heart beating. He let the silence envelop him. Time stood still at the Lake of Three Sorrows. The peaceful retreat was nourishing his body and soul. His private sanctuary was working its magic.

Two weeks had passed since their return from the reunion. Troy was making a determined effort to exercise every day until he was exhausted from the exertion. His leg felt stronger each passing day. The doctors at Togus encouraged him to exercise as much as he was capable of doing. Memories and perspectives of what might have been if he had known of Gail's condition never left his conscience. The advantage of hindsight was hurtful. He should have investigated the situation more thoroughly than he did. He knew how easily things could go wrong in the fog of war, and it angered him that he had so readily accepted the official records at the time of the tragedy.

The visits to Togus were a pleasant change of pace. Cera eagerly looked forward to each trip. She and John had been writing on a regular basis. Once Troy had observed Cera when she was composing a letter to John. There was an expectant exuberance about her that was becoming. Since their return from France she was quieter and more serious than usual. She took long walks around the lake and went swimming every day. Troy noticed a more reflective Cera.

The two canoes Ashley had left behind were in excellent condition and Cera developed an expertise with the crafts that surprised herself. There was a portion of the lake near the western outlet that Ashley had warned them to avoid. It could be dangerous with or without a canoe. The Indian maiden and her two children were lost near that part of the lake. The story of their tragic untimely deaths had been woven into the folklore of the region. Some claimed that their spirits never left the area. On certain nights, the beautiful Indian maiden could be seen, shrouded in mist, near the dangerous outlet weeping mournfully.

One day Cera had received a notice from one of her classmates at college to join her for a trip to Cape Cod. Troy urged her to accept the offer. Her friend drove from northern New Hampshire to pick her up and stayed overnight at the cabin. The next morning, Troy waved good-bye to them as they left the driveway. He was now capable of driving the Wagoneer. Cera made him promise to continue with his exercises and to eat well while she was away.

Letters from old acquaintances had been pouring to him since the tour. Troy spent a lot of time at his old Remington portable typewriter answering the inquiries and reminiscing with buddies. Several days after Cera left, the phone rang while he was at his desk near the fireplace. Thinking it might be Cera checking in he answered: "Hello."

"Troy, this is Beth." There was a hesitancy in her voice.

"Is anything wrong, Beth?" he asked.

"That all depends," she answered with a sigh.

"What is it?"

"I'm calling to let you know that our divorce has been completed. I have the papers in my hand. I must tell you that I'm having second thoughts."

"I don't know how to respond to that remark, Beth," Troy replied, filled with images of happier days together.

"I admit that I've wronged you, and I'm prepared to do anything to make amends. Is there any hope for us, Troy?" It was more of a plea than a question. Troy was unsettled by the frank admission, for Beth was never a person to readily accept blame.

"What can I say? I believe it's too late for us now. If we tried again, it might work for a while, but then all that has come between us would be eating away at any progress we might make. Trust has been lost. I accept some of the blame for our failure. The girls are old enough that they don't need us as much as they did. With just the two of us, I don't believe it would work."

"I was prepared to go along with any answer you gave to my question," confessed Beth. "I had to ask it though. I'm sorry, Troy. There's truth in what you said, but I wanted to ask just the same. How is Cera doing?"

"She has grown into a lovely young lady. She left for a few days at Cape Cod with a friend."

"I'm sorry that I missed Ashley before she left for Canada. I always liked her. It must be beautiful there now."

"It is. I've found the perfect place to spend the rest of my days."

"I wish you well, Troy. I'll sign the papers and send them along to you for your signature. You'll have them shortly…"

"It's for the best. I'm sorry too, Beth. I'm not your enemy and I don't hate you. What we once had is gone. Yesterday can never be repeated. I hope that we can still be friends for the girl's sake. They deserve that and so do we," Troy said.

"I agree. Well, goodnight, Troy. Can you forgive me?" Beth asked softly.

"Yes, I can forgive you, Beth. Give Karen my love. How's she doing carrying the baby?"

"She's doing well and is so happy. You take care."

"I will and you do the same. Goodnight, Beth."

Troy hung the phone up and sat back in his chair wondering if he had been too hasty in rejecting Beth's request for a second chance. All that night his head was filled with memories of happier years they had spent together. From the depths of World War Two to the mountainous campaigns of Korea and then to the stinking jungles of Vietnam he had always had Beth and the girls to come home to. That no longer existed. He was alone. It was inevitable that he mourn the dissolution of a marriage, but the divisions that separated them had grown wider over the years until there was little that united he and Beth except the girls. He remembered and it hurt. He was still searching for meaning in his life and worried that it might allude him, especially at his age.

* * *

Cera and her friend spent several days at Cape Cod swimming on the beach and playing tennis at her friend's family cottage. On the way back to Maine, Cera asked her friend to stop at a small town in Massachusetts near the New Hampshire border. She had spoken briefly to Alan Malone before they left France, obtaining his mother's phone number and street address. Earlier that morning, Cera had called Gail from Cape Cod to see if she was at home.

"Hello, is this Mrs. Malone?" asked Cera, wondering if she was doing the right thing.

"Yes, who's calling?" replied Gail. "I recognize your voice, you're Troy's daughter."

"Yes, this is Cera Hansen, Mrs. Malone. I'm calling to see if I could stop by to speak with you later today. I know that this may sound like an unusual request and I'll understand if you decline, but it's important to me that I talk with you."

"I'll be here all day. I don't get out much. Anytime will be fine with me. What is this about anyway?" asked Gail.

"I prefer to leave that for when I'm with you in person. I'll see you in a couple of hours. A friend is driving me back to Maine so I won't take too long with you."

"I'll be expecting you, Cera. How did you get my phone number?"

"Alan gave it to me the last time I saw him in Normandy."

"I understand," said Gail, her mind running through what Cera might want to discuss with her. "Well, drive carefully."

"Thank you, I'll see you in a while."

Cera and her friend arrived at the small town of Amesbury late morning. A security guard at a construction site gave them directions to Gail's address. It was in an older section of town with large maple and elm trees lining both sides of the street.

The house was a small ranch style with lush flower gardens around the front. A paved walkway led to a set of steps leading to a porch around the side entrance of the house beside the garage. There was an air of orderliness and unpretentious grace in the setting of the home.

Cera's friend promised to wait patiently for as long as necessary. Cera looked about the neat lawn and flower gardens in full bloom. She swallowed hard and held her breath as she rang the doorbell.

"I heard you drive up in the automobile," announced Gail. She looked tired and tense with deep lines about her eyes that showed even though she wore dark glasses. There was an air of suppressed emotions about her. "Please come in, Cera."

"I'm sorry to barge in on you like this. I almost called to cancel out. I pray that I'm not walking into something I have no right to do." Suddenly, Cera regretted her rash behavior.

"I'm not sure I know what you're talking about, Cera. You seem upset and distraught. Please come out to the kitchen. We can sit at the table if you like."

"Any place is fine," replied Cera, following her into an immaculately clean and orderly kitchen. There were several vases of fresh picked roses placed around the room filling it with a sweet fresh smell. "The flowers are beautiful and smell so good."

"I can't enjoy their beauty but I can their nice scent. I grow them in my gardens."

"Has your son returned to his duty station?"

"Yes, Alan had just a few days free, enough to make the trip to France with me." Gail sensed Cera's discomfort. "What can I do for you?"

"The first time I met you in the ladies restroom there was something that attracted me to you, Mrs. Malone."

"I felt something too, you were very kind to a stranger."

"When I talked to Alan I had an even stronger feeling about something I didn't understand," said Cera. Gail was nervously folding and unfolding her hands on top of the table. Cera grasped them in hers and cried desperately: "If I'm wrong please forgive me, but I have to tell you something!"

"I'm listening, child."

"You and Alan have been in my thoughts ever since we met. Days passed and I still could not shake the feeling that something was not as it seemed. One night, I was looking over some of the pictures taken at the reunion. You and Alan were in several of the snapshots. My heart beat wildly when I made the discovery that your son Alan looks exactly like my father when he was that age. I have several of his older pictures with me. I wish I could show them to you but I can't!"

Gail began to cry, quietly, at first. Then she started to breath heavier and gasp for breath. Cera was frightened at the depth of her grief and leaped from her chair to embrace the bereaved lady. "I'm so sorry, Mrs. Malone. I'm so sorry."

Cera was witnessing a catharsis and all she could do was stand helplessly by and hold Gail in her arms to console her, hating her meddling impetuosity. The spell lasted for several minutes. Cera located a box of tissues on the counter and placed them where Gail could touch them. Slowly Gail composed herself and breathed deeply. Finally, a sigh of resignation fell from her trembling lips.

"For all those years I've been a mother and a father to Alan. I tried to fill both roles. It was hard, and I can tell you now, that it can't be done. Alan has been my life and my reason for living." Gail removed her glasses, wiped her sightless eyes, and blew her nose with the tissues. She continued, sitting erect, looking at Cera as if she could see her. The lines in her face around her eyes softened.

"You're a very perceptive young lady, and you have seen through my conspiracy. Even Alan failed to see what you've pointed out. Maybe he knew all along and remained silent, I don't really know."

"Are you the Gail that my father talks in his sleep about and thinks frequently of?"

"Probably."

"Are you the reason he wanted to return to Normandy and England? I know that he was glad to see old friends and buddies, but they were not the main reason he wanted to go back. Echoes from the past were calling him. We never knew what those echoes were saying to him, only that it involved someone by the name of Gail. Are you that Gail?"

"Yes, I'm that Gail," she admitted in a whisper.

Cera bit her tongue and asked the question that she had been holding back since the beginning of her conversation with Gail. She knew it was going to be hurtful.

"Is Alan my father's son?"

"Does your father know that you're doing this?" Gail snapped back at Cera.

"No, I'm doing this so that I can help him find some level of peace and comfort in his life. He deserves that and I intend to help him find it."

"Has he asked you to do this?" Gail asked, nervously fidgeting with her hands again.

"Absolutely not," exclaimed Cera. "If he knew, he would be upset with me. He guards the earlier part of his adult life with a protective silence. I doubt if he ever mentioned anything about you to my mother. He certainly never did to me or my sister."

Gail pushed her chair away from the table and began to walk around the kitchen touching familiar pieces of furniture for direction. A nervous restlessness surged through her body. "Young lady, you've succeeded in invading a very private part of my life that I've shared with no one, especially your father."

"I knew that I was going to hurt you by asking that question," replied Cera helplessly. "I'm sorry, Mrs. Malone. I really did not mean to violate your private world. I was only thinking of my father. My visit has been insensitive and I beg your forgiveness. I retract my question and will leave without another word if you wish."

"I respect that you love your father a great deal and want his happiness. I wish him the same. Please don't leave with anger in your heart. I'll answer your question if you'll promise me to never tell your father. When he learns the truth I want to be the one to tell him." Gail sat heavily in her chair and ran her long sensitive fingers around Cera's face. "You're a lovely girl. I can feel the goodness in your heart."

"I promise to never say a word to dad."

"Alan is your father's son and your half-brother!"

Chapter Sixteen

"I knew it," Cera cried, holding onto Gail. It was not a moment of triumph for Cera, but it did validate the unusual feelings that had plagued her since the reunion. She understood the courage it took for Gail to share her secret with a virtual stranger. Tears ran down her cheeks. The reality of Gail's confession sunk into Cera's conscience, regretting the meddlesome invasion of her privacy. Now that she knew the truth, what was she going to do about it? She had solicited a response from the lady she was holding in her arms that changed the future and possibly complicated it. She and Karen had a half-brother they never knew existed until a few seconds ago!

"Now that you know about me what are you going to do with the knowledge? Don't ask me why I never told your father. Maybe it was fear of rejection by him and his family. An immoral woman making claims that he was her child's father, who would have believed it? Besides, a German artillery shell exploded, blinding me and breaking my arm. I was pregnant at the time. I remained silent and never told your father. Fear of rejection and the thought that he would only pity me filled my heart for a long time. It was a difficult decision to make and I've never been certain that it was a correct one.

"Alan doesn't know. As far as he's concerned his father was a soldier that never came back from the war to us. I did not want to burden him with the truth because he's on his way overseas and I'm frightened for him. He's my life. So don't call me Mrs. Malone, I was never married." Gail slumped in her chair drained of energy, holding her head in her hands. Tense tremors of raw emotion again ran through her body. For the first time in her life, she was ashamed of who she was.

For twenty-six years Gail had carried the burden of her intimate circumstance in silence. Surmounting the obstacles that life presented. She was the personification of courage and strength of character. Cera went around the table and again embraced her.

"I'm so sorry. I had no right to pry into your private world. Please forgive me," Cera pleaded. "I'll keep my promise to you. I wish now that I had curbed my inquisitive nature. I certainly had no intentions of inflicting pain on you, Gail Malone. You've won my admiration. Your courage and grace under horrific circumstances are inspiring."

Gail removed her glasses and wiped her eyes. Tremors still ran through her body. She grabbed Cera's arms and stroked them softly.

"I understand your position, Cera. You had honorable intentions, and I can appreciate that. It's nice that you think enough of your father to approach me with such intimate questions. I'm sure he's a wonderful father. Where do we go from here?"

"I'll keep my promise to you. I've meddled enough with other people's feelings and memories. Other lives are involved too. I've been selfish and thinking only of myself. I'm sorry that I've hurt you. You didn't deserve that," Cera confessed.

"Can you give me your phone number in Maine? Someday I'll tell your father."

Cera gave Gail their address and phone number at the cabin on the Lake of Three Sorrows. Then she realized that a written address was useless to her. Gail moved to the Braille typewriter sitting on a counter in the corner of the kitchen next to the phone and began to type the address and number. When she was finished, she removed the sheet of paper from the typewriter and checked it for accuracy. Cera looked at the sheet and saw a series of dots.

"The first thing I learned to do when I was discharged from the Navy was learn to read Braille. It's the universal method of communicating written words within the blind community," said Gail.

"I'm impressed," noted Cera as a doorbell rang interrupting their conversation.

"Who is it?" Gail called from the kitchen.

"It's Les," replied a male voice from the kitchen entrance. "Is anything wrong?"

"Come in, Les. We're in the kitchen," Gail called, standing up from the table. A middle-aged man in a Massachusetts State Policeman's uniform entered the room. He wore three sergeant stripes on his sleeve.

"I was passing by and stopped to see if you needed anything at the store," announced the sturdily built officer with dark inquiring eyes.

"This is Cera Hansen, an acquaintance from our reunion trip to France. Cera this is Les Aikens, a friend of many years."

"I'm glad to meet you, Sergeant Aikens," said Cera.

"The pleasure is mine, Cera. I can't stop but for a minute," answered Les.

"Cera was just leaving," said Gail, holding out her arms to hug Cera.

"Thank you for your time. I can't leave without telling you how much I admire your unselfish commitment to your son. Good-bye. I'll keep in touch."

"Please do, Cera."

"It's been nice meeting you, Sergeant Aikins," said Cera, letting herself out. She noticed the police cruiser parked beside her friend's automobile at the end of the driveway. She left with a new enthusiasm and a spirit of revelation, for she had discovered the source of her father's anguish. A warm glow filled her heart when Gail told her that, "Alan is your half-brother."

Sergeant Aikens watched the car with New Hampshire plates pull out onto the street. He turned to Gail and said" "Are you sure that everything's all right, Gail? You're as white as a ghost and look as if you just received bad news. I worry about you."

"I know that Les, and I'm grateful for your concern. You worry too much. Remember I survived years before I met you."

"Forgive me, I'm overreacting," replied Les, kissing her on the cheek. "Well, I've got a patrol to continue. I'll see you tonight at six if you're ready to go out to dinner."

"That'll be fine, Les," answered Gail anxious to be alone with her thoughts. "You be careful out there."

"You bet," he answered, turning at the door to look at her. "I still think you're the prettiest girl in town."

"Les, I'm fifty years old!" Gail scolded him. His habit of expressing himself with enthusiasm complimented her more serious nature. She heard the police cruiser leave the street and breathed easier.

Gail went to the refrigerator, poured a glass of iced tea and went in the back yard where she had a screened porch erected. Many of the flowers she raised were in full bloom filling the yard with fresh scents that were pleasing to her. She had lost the ability to see, and from that moment her other senses increased in importance and degrees of efficiency. She was able to distinguish the rich aroma from the roses and the sharp pungent smell of tiger lilies. Her ability to hear also increased many times more than it was before the injury. Various tones were much more pronounced and distinguishable. The senses of taste and touch also became a more important part of her awareness of the world around her. Feeling shapes and textures with her hands allowed her to paint a mental image of the things she explored. At times, the image was as vivid as if she was actually looking at an object.

Gail silently recounted her visit with Cera. The reunion trip had given her a feeling of apprehension that would not go away. She felt that she was living on the edge of imminent disaster. Her greatest fear was that Alan would learn the truth and hate her for what she had done. For several days she had trouble sleeping and eating.

Les had been a good friend. She depended on him more than she should, and now, the relationship was becoming heavy with expectations. They were engaged. She rubbed the engagement ring on her finger, a symbol of his affection for her. She liked and respected him but was uncertain if that equated to being in love with him. Lately he was pressing hard for them to set a date to marry. She was not ready to make that commitment and was having trouble defending her position. Alan liked Les and approved of their marriage plans.

Gail's reasons for declining or evading the issue went deep and she was afraid to analyze them too closely. She kept her private desires and wishes isolated from everyday affairs, and rarely took the time to critically evaluate them. A large part of her still lived in that world of yesterday when she could see like everybody else. The fantasy had become reality and that unreal version of reality was limiting her options for happiness.

Cera's searing questions occupied her mind. They had blown the secrecy she had harbored for years. Did she do the right thing telling Troy's daughter about Alan? Cera was the only other person in the world to know the truth. Gail knew that, at some point in time, she had the responsibility of telling Troy about Alan. Her reason for not contacting him was not as valid now as it was during the traumatic environment when the decision was made. Time had passed so quickly! She prayed for wisdom and guidance to do the right thing for all concerned. She could not deny that Troy was a part of her past. The sound of his voice had brought back all the hopes and dreams that young people like them clung to during the war years. At that explosive time it was all they had!

* * *

Days later, Troy sat on the porch watching the sun go down behind Russell Mountain. It was his favorite time of day. The evening breeze whispered softly through the pine trees. The creatures of the night were beginning to take over the landscape. Owls hooted in the distance and the foxes and coyotes began their irritating high pitched chatter to one another. Cera joined him on the porch, passing him a glass of iced tea. She remained silent about her visit with Gail as she had promised.

"When I picked up the mail there was a newsletter from the veterans of your regiment. They've formed an association of the members that went on the tour. A list of the names and addresses is included," Cera noted casually. She was certain that the information would have a profound effect on her father.

"Is that so, Cera?" Troy asked, trying hard to be nonchalant about it.

"Yes, I left it on your desk by the fireplace. Are you going to Togus tomorrow?"

"I should. Are you going with me?" he asked.

"Yes, John told me that his mother would be there. I'd like to meet her."

"Then we'll go right after breakfast. I expect that by now the doctor will be able to determine if I'm fit to remain on active duty or not. What do you think about submitting my resignation?"

"It's really up to you, Dad. As for me, I'd prefer to see you resign and do those things you've never had a chance to do with your life. Follow your heart. That's advice you gave Karen and me over the years."

"We'll see what tomorrow brings. I think I'll turn in early. I had a good workout splitting wood today. "I'll see you in the morning, Cera."

"Goodnight, Dad," she said, watching him look through the mail on the desk. He picked up the list of names and addresses and took it into his room. Cera knew he would do that. She had been feeling guilty knowing Gail's address and not sharing it with him. The appearance of the list resolved that dilemma. She worried about what he would do when he learns the truth from Gail. Knowledge that he had a son could be shattering to his well-being!

Cera drove the Wagoneer to Togus. Troy went directly to the clinic where the staff had him stand and walk in a straight line without his cane. Troy followed the directions relatively easy. The one thing he could not do yet was hold his good leg in the air and try to jump about without losing his balance. He was determined to continue that exercise until he could do it perfectly.

"You're coming along splendidly, Colonel," Doctor Kelly remarked.

"Is that enough to pass muster for active duty?" asked Troy.

"What do you think?"

He knew that an infantry officer needed more agility than he possessed. "I would flunk myself, Doctor."

"You've made it easy for me, Colonel. Let's give it until the end of summer. Maybe in time you'll improve."

"Should I give you my letter of resignation now?"

"There's a good chance that things won't improve with time. I'm sorry. That's not to say that you can't lead a normal life as a civilian."

"Okay, Doctor. We'll be patient and wait. I have to admit that I'm enjoying myself during this recuperative period. Thanks for your honesty."

"Any time, Colonel."

Cera had accompanied Troy to the clinic to determine how long he would have to wait for the doctors to see him. Then, she accompanied him to the exam room and left to see John Lamprey. A few whistles announced her presence. She smiled and waved to the enthusiastic patients. John was sitting in a wheel chair and turned to see her coming towards him.

"It's always nice to see you, Cera," he said, placing a book he was reading on the table.

She kissed him on the cheek. "How are you doing, John?"

"I've got something to show you but I want to wheel out to the terrace so that these guys in here won't make fun of me." The room erupted in whistles and shouts as Cera pushed John to the screened terrace. It was the patient's way of showing support for one of their own.

John was wearing a bathrobe which concealed his new artificial arm and leg. Matching slippers helped conceal the artificial foot. John was nervous and excited. "Close your eyes, Cera," he requested.

"Okay."

"You can look now," said John after a few seconds of silence. He stood up straight and walked around the chair steadying himself with one hand. It was an accomplishment that required a major effort on his part. She appreciated how much determination and discipline it took for John to reach this level of achievement.

"I'm so proud of you, John," she exclaimed feeling like shouting.

"I've got something else to show you," he announced with a triumphant grin.

He took three steps toward the balcony rail without support. He moved the artificial leg as if it was his own. They were deliberate mechanical steps that with time and practice would give John mobility as if he had both legs. He turned to look at Cera. Her approval was important to him.

John turned to a bouquet of roses in a small blue vase sitting on the terrace railing. His movements were slow, methodical and somewhat unsteady, but he successfully plucked one rose from the vase by clasping the stem with the small serrated tong located at the end of his new arm where his hand would have been. He offered the rose to Cera: "A pretty rose for a pretty girl."

Cera burst into tears accepting the rose he held out to her. It was a triumph of the human spirit. She embraced John and kissed him on the lips. It was a natural instinct. He wrapped both of his arms around her.

"You've been doing wonderful since I last saw you," she cried, flushed with emotions.

"I couldn't have done it without your support."

"John, you're just being modest. I can't believe how far you've progressed since you came to Togus. I appreciate how much hard work has gone into your accomplishments. I'm so proud of you," she said, backing away from John so that he could return to the wheelchair. "How much longer will they keep you here at the hospital?"

"About two more weeks," he answered. Cera's reaction to his efforts made all the work worthwhile.

An orderly stepped out on the terrace announcing that John had another visitor, his mother. He looked down the hallway leading to the terrace and saw his mother approaching. She was a small petite woman with dark hair wearing a pink dress. A young girl Cera's age accompanied her.

"Here come my mother and an old high school friend,"

"I'll let you visit with them in private, John."

"No, please stay," pleaded John. "I want you to meet my mom. I've talked to her about you and your father."

"If you don't mind," said Cera.

John's mother hugged him in a flourish. "You're looking so much better, John," she cried in a tremulous voice. She noticed the artificial arm and touched the tong at the end. Her voice was filled with pride: "John, you're wearing it already."

"Mom, I'm beginning to use it and my leg too. Before we get into that I want to introduce you to Cera Hansen. Cera, this is my mother. The lady with her is an old friend, Joyce Almond."

Joyce brushed past Cera and kissed John. Cera felt uncomfortable. It was as if she was laying claim to John. She was a tall slender young woman with light brown hair pulled back behind her ears. She turned to meet Cera.

Mrs. Lamprey smiled at Cera. "Hello, Cera. John has talked a lot about you and your father,"

"Hello, Joyce," said Cera. "John has come a long ways since we first met in Hawaii." Then, she turned toward his mother. "I'm pleased to have a chance to meet you, Mrs. Lamprey."

"Each time I've been here I've missed you," said Mrs. Lamprey. "Thank you for helping, John. I'm glad we had a chance to meet."

"I was just about to leave when you arrived. I'll see you on our next trip, John," said Cera, holding the rose in her hand. "You've made remarkable progress. My father will be pleased to hear about it. Nice meeting you. Joyce." Cera walked away feeling that something important was left unsaid between her and John. She went directly to the Wagoneer and sat behind the wheel. She wrapped the rose in a tissue and placed it in her pocket. The discovery of feelings for John was not unexpected. Joyce's performance made her feel insignificant like an intruder and it bothered her.

Troy left the clinic satisfied with his recovery and the patient way the decision to terminate his military career was being handled. He saw Cera in the Wagoneer and was puzzled at the dejected look on her face.

"Is anything wrong, Cera?"

"No. I just left when John's mother and an old girlfriend came to see him. I felt as if I was in the way."

"That doesn't sound like John. Did he tell you that?"

"Not in those same words. He's making great progress learning how to use his new leg and arm. He picked a rose out of a vase while I was there."

"Well, that does sound like progress."

"That lady coming out the door is his mother," interrupted Cera. "She seems to be looking for someone." Mrs. Lamprey saw Cera and Troy in the vehicle and started walking towards them.

"I'm sorry to intrude," exclaimed Mrs. Lamprey, addressing Troy directly. She seemed upset about something. "May I take the liberty of introducing myself? I'm Marla Lamprey, John's mother."

"I'm Troy Hansen and am glad to meet you, Mrs. Lamprey. Your son is a brave soldier. You and your husband must be very proud of him," said Troy, shaking her hand. She was an attractive lady. At a distance her petite figure made her look more like a school girl than a middle age mother. Her large brown eyes blinked occasionally when she talked and she moved her hands expressively.

"John's father was killed at Bastogne," Marla Lamprey hesitated a second and continued: "I wanted to ask your advice about something. Your daughter has been more influential to John's recovery than she thinks. I'm grateful for that, Cera."

"He's a fine young man and deserves a lot of credit," Cera answered, anxious to hear what John's mother had to say.

"Yes, I'm very proud of him. Colonel Hansen, I wanted to ask you some questions about John."

"I'll be glad to help in any way I can."

"John has confided in me that he is anxious to become proficient with his artificial limbs so that he can get behind the controls of a helicopter and fly again. I'm pleased to hear him think positively of the future, but the thought of him in the cockpit of a helicopter flying again frightens me."

"Your son has set an exacting goal for himself, Mrs. Lamprey. I'd encourage him to pursue it with all the vigor and determination he possesses," Troy suggested without reservation.

"Wouldn't it be dangerous for him?"

"If he's able to pass the tests for a civilian license I don't see how it is any more dangerous than you driving your automobile home tonight," Troy mentioned, defending John's goals.

"Doesn't he want to continue with his teaching career?" asked Cera, evaluating every word being spoken.

"Yes, he wants to get back in the classroom to teach. I teach English at the same school. He was very popular with the students. The flying thing has become an obsession with him and it still frightens me. I appreciate your thoughts, Colonel. Thank you for your time."

"Don't forget, Mrs. Lamprey. Your son was trained in the best helicopter school in the world by the United States Army. I personally can vouch for their remarkable skills and competence," said Troy forcefully.

"John knew that I was coming out to speak to you. I was afraid you may have already left. The doctors said that I can take him home for the weekend. It'll be the first time since he was commissioned two years ago. He asked me to extend an invitation for you to join us for the weekend, Cera. We have plenty of room for you at home. It seemed important to John and I'm interested in anything that will help my son recover."

"Oh my, Mrs. Lamprey. What about Joyce? I don't want to interfere."

"Nonsense my child, Joyce came down in her own car to see John. They were close friends in high school and dated occasionally. Now that he's won the Medal of Honor she wanted to become a part of his life. They got along fine but I always thought of her as a spoiled brat! She took a close look at John's limitations, especially his arm, and asked if he could hide the metal tong that will replace his hand. It offended her elevated sensibilities. They had words over it and she left shortly after you walked out, Cera."

Troy listened and watched Cera as John's mother spoke. "I can drive now. If you want to accept Mrs. Lamprey's invitation I'll be fine. I just may take a ride to Massachusetts for the rest of the day," said Troy.

"All right, Daddy. I'll be glad to accept, Mrs. Lamprey. I'll see you later, Dad. Maybe you can pick me up when we bring John back to Togus," replied Cera.

"I'm so glad I caught you in time," said Mrs. Lamprey excitedly. She searched through her small purse and took out a small note pad. "I'll give you our address and phone number, Colonel, in case you need to get in touch with Cera."

"Thank you," replied Troy, accepting the piece of paper and placing it in his pocket. He hugged Cera and looked into her eyes. She was happy. He squeezed her and turned to John's mother. "It has been nice meeting you, Mrs. Lamprey. I wish you and John all the best. I'll be in touch with you Cera before the end of the week."

"Good luck on your trip to Massachusetts, Dad," said Cera, leaving with Mrs. Lamprey. Their eyes met for a split second. She knew where he was going!

Chapter Seventeen

U. S. Highway Route One was a road Troy had used frequently over the years. It went through Amesbury, Massachusetts. When Mrs. Lamprey invited Cera to her home for the weekend, he was relieved. It left him free to seek an opportunity to speak to Gail. There was an element of urgency, even desperation that drove him to see her again. The list of names and addresses of those present at the reunion had included Gail's in Amesbury. He was in more emotional turmoil now than before leaving for the tour and his need for answers to questions was increasing in intensity. Once Troy learned the truth of what happened, he could put the past to rest and start life anew.

Appearing at her doorstep unannounced would be insensitive on his part so he called her from a filling station in Hampton, New Hampshire a couple of towns north of Amesbury.

Hello," Gail answered the phone.

"Gail, this is Troy. I'm calling from Hampton. I'd like to talk to you if that's all right with you?" he asked breathlessly.

"I had a feeling that when the list of names and addresses was circulated I'd be hearing from you, Troy," she mentioned, relieved that it had actually happened.

"Is this a bad time?" he asked, his hand holding the phone was shaking. The voice he remembered so well had not changed.

"No," she answered without hesitation. "If you come along now we can be alone to talk. Are you sure you want to do this, Troy?"

"How can you ask that question, Gail? Nothing in my life has been the same since I lost you. Knowing that you survived the war and avoided me is driving me out of my mind. Since the reunion I've thought of nothing else. Could you give me directions to your home? I'm about five miles from the New Hampshire/Massachusetts state line on Route One."

She gave him precise directions to her doorstep. A half hour later he was parking in the driveway of her home, a bundle of uncontrollable nerves. Gail had heard the Wagoneer pull up to the house. It had a unique engine sound. Now that she had heard it she would be able to distinguish it in the future. Sounds to her were like signatures to those who were not blind.

"Come in, Troy," she called from the entrance. He was wearing his tan uniform without a tunic. It was hot and humid and he was perspiring even in the lightweight uniform.

"I'd forgotten how humid New England can be," he said, stepping into her kitchen. Gail wore a light blue blouse with a pair of jeans. She had been working in one of her flower gardens when he called. She was as attractive as ever. His heart pounded just being near her. "It's nice to see you again, Gail. I hesitated several times on my way down here, almost turning back once. I've had the feeling that you would not want to receive me. My first thoughts upon seeing you in England was to thank God. My prayers had been answered. My joy was beyond control until I came face to face with an air of indifference, even anger, which flowed from you. I don't understand why. When we parted in France I had the distinct impression that you were glad to be rid of me without knowing why. I found it hard to accept."

"I've fixed some iced tea. It goes good on these kind of days. We can take it out back on my porch where we'll be private and comfortable."

"Iced tea will be fine."

They walked through a sitting room onto a small screened porch well shaded by large elm trees. Gail sat self-consciously on a wicker chair with a coffee table between her and the chair Troy took. He watched every step she made and marveled at the ease in which she moved around the furniture and fixtures.

"I'm glad that you've come, Troy. Every night since the reunion has been a sleepless one for me too. I owe you some explanations. It's only fair," she paused to collect her thoughts, looking at Troy as if she could see him. "If you'll be patient with me I'll try to answer your questions. So much has transpired that I don't know where to begin. Before I continue, you must know that my concern for your welfare dictated most of my actions."

"I'm not here to stand in judgment of you. I've prayed so often for a chance to see you and let you know what was in my heart."

"I hear you, Troy."

"What did I do wrong, Gail? I believed that you were killed in an artillery barrage. Records that I checked gave no evidence that you were alive. All I could do was assume that you were gone forever!"

"I'm sorry, Troy," Gail could feel the turmoil that motivated him. "My burns and broken arm were readily treatable. My hearing is not as good as it once was, so if I don't understand you, talk slower and more distinctly. I tried a hearing aid. It made me feel even less secure because sounds were not natural. I have something to share with you that has been a burden to me all the years since the war. If you view me as a different person from the nurse you once knew, it's because I have changed. I'm blind, almost fifty years old and I'm frightened of the future. Back then I was ready to take on the world."

"We've all changed, Gail. What has burdened you for years?" Troy asked, uncertain if he wanted to know the answer.

Gail sat back in her chair, took a sip of her iced tea and began to tell Troy what had happened to her. Several days after D-Day at Normandy, Gail was notified that she was about to be reunited with her Naval unit off the Normandy coast. She was relieved of duty and had collected her records at the Army battalion clearing center close to the front lines. Just as she was leaving the tent, she was near the center of a large explosion. Her hair was burned off and her left arm was broken in several places. Her entire body was covered with lesions and cuts, and she was blind. The quick actions of a jeep driver probably saved her life from the burning crater. He and his passenger grabbed her and rushed to an aid center a mile closer to the coast. No information existed of her treatment until long after the war when the records for the unit were collected in the Federal archives. The Army and Navy had listed her as a victim of the massive barrage that destroyed the medical clearing station. Her name had not been removed from the roster list because the clerk was not on duty when she was relieved.

"I did not contact you after the war or meet you at the Wentworth By The Sea Hotel because I was in and out of several hospitals and I was blind. I did not want you to pity me."

"Gail," cried Troy, controlling his anger. "Didn't you know me well enough that your blindness would not have made one whit of a difference to me?"

"I did treat you shabbily at the reunion and I apologize for my rudeness. Alan was with me."

"Why should his presence make any difference? We could have excused ourselves at anytime to talk in private," Troy argued, forcefully.

"We could have, but at the time I was very unsettled by the prospect of meeting you again. You're not the only one who cherished old memories," she said, turning away from Troy. She wiped her eyes underneath the dark glasses.

"What are you trying to say?"

"In my own nervous way, I'm trying to tell you that when I was wounded, I was also pregnant!"

The words erupted in Troy's conscience like a bomb. "Pregnant???" he exclaimed.

"Yes, Troy," she answered with trembling lips. "That last night we were together at that English inn…"

"Gail, are you telling me that Alan is my son?" Troy made the statement and wondered if he was dreaming. It sounded ludicrous! Twenty-five years after the fact he learns that he has a son. He stood up and nervously began walking around the porch. He knew that there was a logical explanation for Gail's sudden reappearance in his life. "Why didn't you tell me, Gail? Why? I can't believe you did not let me know about your condition."

Gail was crying. She knew that he would be angry, and she did not blame him. She would have lived the rest of her life without telling him if Cera had not discovered the truth. Troy deserved better than that. She was ashamed of her deception.

145

"The only excuse I can give you Troy is that I did not want you to feel obligated to me or the child."

"My God, Gail! How could you come to such a cruel decision as that? If I'm Alan's father I was already obligated," Troy said, trying to keep his voice down.

"Yes, I know that, Troy. It was not an easy decision. My blindness, at that time, was something I had a hard time accepting. I didn't want you to feel sorry or pity me either," sobbed Gail. "I was frightened of rejection and possible derision from your family and friends."

"Didn't you know me better than that? I loved you with every fiber in my body, Gail. Nothing mattered except you. How could you not know that?" he questioned.

"I was wrong. Your anger is justified. I had always planned to tell you some time. As the years went by I assumed that you had married, and that kind of news would have been unsettling for a married couple, so I remained silent and the years rolled by."

"I did marry. We had two girls. Cera my younger daughter was on the tour with us. You had met her in a restroom."

"Yes, she's a remarkable girl. I made Cera promise to not say anything to you until I had a chance to tell you face to face."

"You mean Cera knew about this?" Troy was upset that his daughter knew before he did. "What kind of a conspiracy is Cera a part of?"

"Let me explain, Troy. Cera had pictures of Alan and myself taken at the tour. She compared his picture with one of you as a younger soldier and noticed the similarities. She's an intelligent young lady. I asked her to not tell you because I wanted to do that myself."

"When?"

"It would have been soon, Troy, believe me. I've been a little upset about his new duty station. He's at Fort Dix, New Jersey and was scheduled for Vietnam again. The last time he called he said it was changed. He's now going to Germany. Alan has a right to know who his father is."

"I'm surprised he hasn't insisted on knowing before this," Troy replied, shaken by the revelations.

146

"He's asked all right. I kept putting him off the best I could. I did not want to outright lie to him. As far as he's concerned his father was a soldier in World War Two. Shortly after the war my parents passed away. They were modest hard-working people. Their only asset was the family home which I sold and moved to Amesbury. I was an only child. Alan grew up in a community that did not know who I was. I started using Mrs. Malone to protect him and to stop inquiring tongues. To those who asked about his father, I told them the same thing I told Alan and let it go at that. People can draw their own conclusions. I became a recluse of sorts because of my blindness."

"My God, Gail. All of that could have been avoided if you had contacted me. I can't forgive you for not trusting me more. I needed you then more than you needed me. What a waste all those years have been." Troy exclaimed in a loud voice.

"Are you happy now with your wife and family?" Gail asked, anxious to change the focus of their conversation away from her.

"My wife and I are going through a divorce now. She's found someone else. Our older girl, Karen, is pregnant and living in California. I'll be a grandfather soon. Cera is going to college at the University of New Hampshire, but you must already know that." There was an element of sarcasm in his voice.

"I'm sorry I asked," Gail replied in a wavering voice, holding her head in her hands. All of a sudden life seemed more complicated for her. It was hard for her to believe that she was having this conversation with Troy. Considering the gravity of the news he had just digested, he was relatively calm. His gentle disposition had not changed she thought. A doorbell at her front door interrupted the overloaded silence that filled the air. She asked whoever it was to come in.

"It's me, Les. Are you all right, Gail?" asked an authoritative voice.

"I'm on the porch, Les," answered Gail.

The policeman was surprised to confront Troy, an Army Colonel sitting on the porch with Gail. "I didn't recognize the vehicle outside and thought I should stop by."

147

"Les this is Colonel Troy Hansen, an old friend. Troy this is Les Aiken, a new friend."

"I'm pleased to meet you, Colonel."

"It's my pleasure, Sergeant," said Troy, shaking his strong hand. The two men silently appraised each other.

"I can't stop for long. Do we still have a date for tomorrow?" asked Les.

"Yes, if you're going to be off duty."

"I will be," answered Les, kissing Gail on the cheek. "Nice meeting you, Colonel. Have a good day."

"You too, Sergeant," said Troy, watching the policeman leave the porch. He was upset observing the level of intimacy that passed between them. "You're well protected now."

"Les has been good to me. We're engaged and go out occasionally," she explained quickly. The level of uneasiness that developed between the two men was perceived by Gail.

"Tell me how it has been for you, Gail? How have you gotten along over the years?"

"I've had a relatively good life considering everything. My Navy disability payment is not enough for me to live on so I decided, before the war ended, that I'd have to join the work world. The Navy sent me to Braille school where I mastered the blind person's typewriter. I was lucky I had taken typing in high school and nursing school. I was able to obtain a teaching certificate. I teach history and civics at the local high school. It supplements my income and gives me a sense of achievement. The school has been good for me. Alan was in one of my classes. Tell me, Troy, what did you do on November 4, 1945?"

"I was able to get a few days off and went to Wentworth-By-The-Sea Hotel and sat on the porch all day. I had a feeling that you were with me but I was really alone. I left the hotel and drove to Buzzard's Bay where I looked up your picture in the high school yearbook at the local library. I also drove by where your parents lived believing that contacting them would have been painful for everybody. It was in the evening and I ate at a restaurant in the middle of the town sitting at a booth near the exit door. I remember talking about the war with the cashier."

"I knew that was you!" she cried in disbelief. "I was sitting in one of the booths near the check-out register. I remember hearing a voice that sounded like you. I dismissed it, my imagination was working on overtime then. It was a horrible day for me, if that's any consolation to you. I was six months pregnant then."

"When was Alan born?"

"February 15, 1946. You can figure it out. It was nine months to the day after our last night together on the Isle of Wright."

"I'm not doubting your word, Gail. I'm just having trouble comprehending the fact that I have a son. Have you ever mentioned me to him?'

"Not until we met on the tour. Then, I simply called you an old friend, which was true."

"I noticed that you had a first lieutenant bar pinned to your hat that first time we met in England on the tour."

"If you remember I pinned your captain bars on your uniform and kept the first lieutenant bars. They were important to me. For years I carried them with me everywhere I went. Our son is wearing them now. I pinned them on his uniform when we were in France on the tour. He's a fine young man. I'm so proud of him. Ever since he was a little boy he's wanted to go to West Point. During his senior year in high school he took the exam and was accepted. He could have taken any branch he wanted at graduation time, his grades were high. The infantry has always had an appeal to him. That fact frightens me."

"A son from West Point," repeated Troy, smiling. "Did you know that he confronted me in the hallway of the hotel asking about my relationship with you? He was worried for you. He was most respectful to me but there was no doubt in my mind that he was prepared to risk his career in the Army to defend you. I'd say you did well by him, Gail."

"He did that to you?" Gail smiled and chuckled. Troy recalled how she would do that sometimes when she was pleased about something.

"What are his orders now? I'm on medical leave and have plenty of time on my hands. I intend to look him up and explain who I am. He's entitled to know that. I also owe him an explanation why I was not there for him over the years. If I had known I would have been."

"The judgment call I made was not a good one," admitted Gail, grasping for his hand.

Troy felt the long sensitive fingers against his wrist and tremors ran like lightening through his body. She had risen from the ashes of the war and lived in his memory for years. Now, he finds that she was engaged to marry a policeman. That fact prevented his imagination from going any further. Instead, he concentrated on Alan.

"Where do we go from here, Gail?" he asked, searching for some direction for the future. He had to see Alan. "Does Cera know that Alan is her half-brother?"

"Yes, I told her a few days ago. She was very quiet about it. I heard you using a cane when you came into the house. How bad are your injuries, Troy?"

"The bullet punctures are about all healed. My leg is going to be all right. I'll probably have a limp. I don't mind. It could have been worse. I'm lucky to be alive. My Army career will be finished, but I've already accepted that."

"You deserve to live a normal life without the threat of combat. Your family must be pleased that you'll be able to relax at home."

"Where's Alan stationed?" Troy asked a second time. She seemed reluctant to want to tell him.

"Troy, I'm afraid that if you confront him with the truth he'll feel that I've deceived him all those years," Gail cried, nervously playing with her empty ice tea glass.

"What do you suggest?" Troy asked, noting her anxiety.

"Are you prepared to see Alan on a short notice?"

"Yes, within twenty-four hours. Cera is with a wounded soldier and his family near Bar Harbor, Maine for the weekend. "I could drive to Fort Dix from here in three or four hours," responded Troy.

"I don't have the right to ask anything of you," explained Gail hesitantly. "May I go with you when you tell Alan that you're his father? It would mean a lot to me. I'm responsible for keeping him uninformed. Will you take me with you?"

"I could never refuse you anything, Gail."

Chapter Eighteen

Troy copied Alan's address, which contained his battalion designation, in a small notebook he always carried with him. Over the course of his career in the Army Troy had been in and out of Fort Dix several times. He knew the facility well. It was primarily used as a staging area and training command.

"May I use your phone, Gail? I want to call base headquarters to determine his status."

"It's on the kitchen counter, Troy," she said, filled with misgivings and apprehension about what was taking place. "I'll show you." She walked in the kitchen and pointed to the phone.

Troy dialed information for the Base number and had them ring it for him. A young voice answered.

"Fort Dix Army Base. How may I help you? This is Corporal Abbott."

"Corporal Abbott this is Colonel Troy Hansen. Could you tell me the name of the Officer of the Day at Headquarters?"

"Yes, Sir. It's Major Peter Ryan. Do you want me to connect you to his office?"

"Please do Corporal, thank you."

"Major Ryan here," Troy was in luck. Ryan was an old acquaintance. Their paths had crossed several times in the course of their careers in the Army. "Pete Ryan this is Troy Hansen."

"Troy or I should say Colonel. I saw your name on the latest promotion list and was glad to know that you made bird colonel. Congratulations, it's well deserved."

"Thanks Pete, I've got a favor to ask of you. Without going into a lot of detail I'd like to be able to speak to First Lieutenant Alan Malone. It's important to me and very personal. He's with the 98th Regiment First Battalion. Can you help me?"

"I'll try, Colonel. Give me a few seconds to check on the unit training schedules. We've been pretty active lately. Malone's battalion is assigned to an old friend of yours, Colonel Bud Touraine. Hold the line for a second," said Major Ryan.

"If Bud Touraine is taking them to Vietnam, or Germany they've got the best."

"Okay, Troy. The first battalion has just come out of the field for the day. If you want to hold the line open I'll try to locate Lieutenant Malone and you can talk directly to him."

"I'll hold. Thanks, Pete." Troy held a hand over the mouthpiece and spoke to Gail. "An old friend answered. He's trying to locate Alan. Why don't you speak to him? I certainly don't want to get into things over the phone."

"I agree, I'll talk with him," agreed Gail.

"Pete, can you hear me?"

"I hear you, Troy. I'm ringing the battalion command post now."

"Pete could you not tell him that it was me who initiated the phone call? It's important."

"I understand, Troy."

"Tell him that his mother wants to talk to him. She's standing beside me."

"Roger, I have Lieutenant Malone on the line and will connect you to him."

"Hello?" answered Alan.

"Alan, this is me calling."

"Is anything wrong, Ma?" he asked in a stern tone.

"No nothing is wrong, Alan. Listen, I want to see you before you ship out. Would you be able to spend some time with me tomorrow? I know this sounds unusual, Son, but bear with me, please."

"How would you get here? Is Les bringing you?"

"We have a dinner date for tomorrow," Gail explained. "He won't be bringing me. Alan, please don't press me for information I'm not prepared to give you over the phone. There's no emergency and I'm fine. What's so unusual about a mother wanting to see her son again? Don't worry, I'll be in good hands."

"Would this have anything to do about the tour we took, Ma? This request is out of character, but I'll trust you. I've got a desk full of paper work waiting for me. I'll be at the battalion command post all day. If I ask my Commanding Officer for some time off when you arrive I'm sure it will be granted. He's a top-notch CO."

"I'm glad you like him. I'll be there tomorrow. If schedules can't be worked out I'll call to leave word. Take care, I love you Son."

"I love you too, Ma. I'll be here when you arrive."

Gail shared the things Alan said with Troy.

"I'm sure he'll like Colonel Touraine. He's a soldier's soldier. I served with him in Korea."

"What do we do now, Troy?" asked Gail nervously.

"First, I've got to call my daughter, Cera. I should let her know what I'm doing and that I won't be able to pick her up. Was she shocked when you told her about Alan?"

"No, she had already figured it out and confronted me for confirmation."

"That sounds like Cera. May I use your phone?"

"Please do," replied Gail.

"Hello, Mrs. Lamprey. This is Troy Hansen. Could I please speak to Cera?"

"She and John are on the porch, I'll get her," said Mrs. Lamprey in a calm voice.

"Are you all right, Dad?" Cera asked anxiously.

"I'm fine, Cera. I just wanted to let you know that I can't pick you up at Togus as planned."

"That will work out well. Mrs. Lamprey is going to take me back tomorrow before she drops John off at Togus. I've talked so much about home that John is anxious to see where we live. I'm not going to ask where you're going, Dad, but is this pertaining to someone who was on the tour with us?" asked Cera. She detected an air of uncertainty in her father's voice. Did he already know about Alan?

"We'll talk when I get back. Trust me, Honey."

"You know I do. I just don't want you to get hurt anymore. You be careful."

"I promise. I love you, Cera."

153

"I love you too, Daddy. I pray that this journey you are taking will resolve the turmoil that has always been just below the surface in your life. I'll keep the home fires burning while you're away," Cera told him and hung up.

"You certainly handled that diplomatically," Gail said, hearing every word between them.

Troy looked at his watch, it was three thirty PM. "Are you prepared to leave right away? "It'll be as quick and as easy to drive door to door as it would be to fly."

"God in Heaven," cried Gail. "I wish this trip wasn't necessary. If Alan was not going overseas again, I'd wait for a more opportune time. He's got enough worries on his mind now, and I don't want to upset him with unanswered questions he always asks."

"Then your explanation is compelling enough to make the trip without delay. What is gained in waiting except a longer period of anxiety?"

"I can leave in fifteen minutes. Are you prepared to do this on such a short notice, Troy?"

"I've been a soldier for almost thirty years moving from place to place with little warning. It has become a way of life with me. I always have an emergency shaving kit and extra uniform packed for such occasions. They're in the Wagoneer. What will you do about Lester?" wondered Troy.

"I had forgotten about that," she said. "Well, it'll just have to wait until we return. I'll call him."

"While you're doing that, I'll get the Wagoneer filled with gas and check the tires. That'll give you some privacy. I'll be back shortly. Don't rush, we have plenty of time."

"I'll be ready when you get back."

Troy's steps were lighter as he walked toward the Wagoneer and drove to the nearest service station. The anxieties that had plagued him for a long time were slowly disappearing. He could do nothing about events of the past, but he was in a position to influence elements of his future. He had a son. That fact buoyed his spirits.

Gail called Les as soon as Troy left the house. She had his vehicle number. He answered on the first ring.

"Hello."

"Les, this is Gail. I wanted to let you know that I'm on my way to Fort Dix to see Alan. I'll call you when I get back."

"Who's taking you there?"

"Troy Hansen," she answered without any explanation.

"I'm not sure I understand what's going on, Gail. Will you be safe with this stranger?" Les had a tendency to treat her as if she was helpless. She also detected a defensiveness that she had not experienced in their relationship of a few years. "I could take you to Fort Dix tomorrow. I've got the day off."

"Thanks for the offer Les, but I'm going with Colonel Hansen. I'm not in a position to explain right now," she replied firmly.

"Are you going to stay overnight?"

"Probably," she answered irritably. She was not in the habit of being questioned the way he was doing. "Les, I'm not a child, I'm a mature woman and I've made up my mind to do this thing. It means a lot to me. That's all I can tell you right now. I'll see you when I get back. Good-bye."

"Good-bye, Gail."

Gail was sitting on the porch with a suitcase beside her when Troy turned into the driveway.

"I was just thinking, Troy. Are you going to be able to drive all the way to Fort Dix and back with your leg?"

"I can walk short distances now without my cane. I'm getting stronger everyday. The Jeep is an automatic, so I don't have to use both legs. May I escort you to the Wagoneer?" asked Troy, placing her right hand on his left arm.

"Yes," she answered. "Since we're going to be together for a while, I'd like to go over a few things with you before we start. First, I'm not a cripple. I'm only blind. I'm capable of doing more things than you might imagine. When we're walking together, I feel more secure holding your arm like I am now. As long as the way is free of obstructions I'll be fine. If there are steps or other objects in the way warn me about them in relation to the way we are facing. Directly ahead of my face is twelve o'clock, my outstretched right arm is three o'clock, my left arm is nine o'clock. My back is six o'clock."

"I understand, Gail. Do you ever use a white cane?"

"Yes," she replied, reaching in the purse slung over her shoulder. She pulled out a white aluminum rod and released a spring on the handle. It opened up to a sturdy three foot cane with a lanyard on the handle. "I use it when I'm alone. When I'm with someone it's easier to fold it away and walk with them."

"I notice an element of independence. I saw that in you years ago."

Troy opened the Wagoneer passenger door for Gail and made sure her hands and feet were away from the door jamb before closing it. He placed her hand on the door handle.

"I'm all set now."

"Just one more thing, Gail. Feel down beside the seat with your right hand. You'll feel a webbed seat belt. Bring it around you and connect it to the other end of the belt on your left side." She did as directed. "Now you're ready to travel safely."

They rode in silence for several miles. Troy had checked the route they needed to travel, estimating the distance to be about two hundred and fifty miles. Five hours of travel time on the expressways should bring them to Fort Dix.

"We'll be going through Hartford in about an hour. What do you say if we stop the other side of Hartford for a bite to eat? That will give the out-of-work-traffic a chance to wind down."

"I haven't eaten much today, so that will be fine as far as I'm concerned," answered Gail. Her mind was preoccupied with the message they were bringing to Alan. She was especially worried that he might consider her a cheap immoral woman, or possibly, he would be relieved to learn the identity of his father. She realized that she knew very little about Troy since the war. "Tell me about yourself, Troy. Has life been good to you?"

"My life has been what I made of it, Gail. It took me a long time to accept the fact that you were gone. You'll never know how much I needed you. When the war ended, I had no other place to go, so I stayed in the Army. I don't regret that decision, but the constant moves from post to post over the years were hard on the family. Beth especially disliked that part of it, tolerating it for the kids and for me. Now that they are capable of taking care of themselves, she saw a chance to get out from under it. I don't blame her. There wasn't very much there for either of us."

"Cera seems to be a wonderful girl. She touched me with her warmth and sincerity that first time I met her in the washroom," explained Gail.

"She's a special girl like her sister Karen. What else would a proud dad say?" Troy chuckled softly. "The girls have made my life worthwhile. Beth and I had reached the end of the road. I don't hate her for the breakup. If she can find happiness with someone else, I wish her luck. The girls are very close to her. Living a lie is no fun."

"I can relate to that. Alan told me that you wore ribbons for the Distinguished Service Medal and the Silver and Bronze Stars. He was impressed."

"The Army has been good to me. I have no regrets. I'm sure I'll soon be discharged with some medical disability. I've already made up my mind to retire. I just recently purchased a place in north central Maine. It's an isolated log cabin on a lake. Both Cera and I are real happy with the purchase. She's been with me since school let out in June. She flew to Pearl Harbor to be with me at the Army hospital."

"I have the impression that she's taking good care of Dad."

"I can't treat her like a little girl anymore," Troy laughed. "She's grown up since I last saw her. I'd like to hope that I've grown some too."

"Personal growth is a continuous process. Without it we grow old fast."

They passed through Hartford heading towards Danbury. Troy saw a sign for a steak house restaurant at the next exit and left the highway. "I'm ready for a steak. How about you, Gail?"

"I can eat steak at home and like it. In public places I have to be careful what I order. I can't gracefully cut a steak into small pieces. Soups and sandwiches are easier to eat without drawing attention to myself."

"I hadn't thought of that," mused Troy.

"It's easier for blind people to eat food from a bowl instead of a flat plate unless we can use our fingers to touch the food. I've learned to live with the limitations. I could have been killed and never have known the joy of our son."

"I say you've been a courageous lady who deserves a lot of credit. In that respect you haven't changed, Gail."

"If you don't stop with the compliments, I'll get a swelled head," she laughed. It was the first time he had heard her do that in twenty-five years.

They ate a leisurely dinner. Troy ordered his steak. Gail stuck with a vegetable soup and a ham sandwich. Troy insisted in cutting up some of his steak into small pieces and putting it in her soup bowl. She laughed softly again when she told him how good it tasted.

Four hours later Troy pulled into a motel at the outskirts of the large Fort Dix Army base. Gail had reclined her bucket seat and was resting. When he stopped she sat up.

"Where are we?"

"Close to the base in central New Jersey. We should put up here for the night so that we'll be well rested for the day ahead of us. The vacancy sign is on. I'll go in and get two rooms for us."

"All right," Gail said, approving the logic of his statement.

Ten minutes later he returned to walk Gail to her room. He flicked on the light for himself realizing that it made no difference to her. He patiently waited for her to familiarize herself with the room and private bath. Her first priority was to draw a mental map of the four walls and adjoining bathroom. Troy got her suitcase and placed it on the baggage table, directing her hand to it.

"Thank you for being so kind, Troy. I'm tired and a good night's sleep is in order for both of us."

"I'm in the room adjoining the wall of your bed. If you need me for anything, pound on the wall with your fist or a shoe. Goodnight, Gail. I'll lock the door on my way out." He placed two fingers under her chin and bent to kiss her. She lifted her lips to his.

Chapter Nineteen

First Lieutenant Malone reported to his battalion Command Post early the next morning. He had slept very little thinking of the things his mother had not said. Her phone call did nothing to inspire positive thinking on his part. Never in his life had he questioned his mother's statement that his father was a soldier. Who he was and what kind of person were questions she persistently refused to answer and outright dismissed as irrelevant. It had bothered him in high school, for his friends and neighbors wondered more than he who the man was. West Point sharpened his awareness of fathers because the military community was a large family. Sons that followed in their father's footsteps made lineage a sacred factor. He was never satisfied or comfortable answering the question "who's your father?" His friends praised or berated their fathers. He ended up playing dumb. He had always felt cheated.

His battalion commander told him that he had a visitor at the reception center near the main gate and that he was excused from duty for the rest of the day. Alan jumped into the battalion's Jeep giving the driver instructions to take him to the visitor's center. He saw his mother talking to a bird colonel and hurried to her side confronting Colonel Hansen with a worried look on his face.

"Hi, Ma," greeted Alan, giving her a hug. "You got here earlier than I expected. I've been excused for the day. Would you like to come to my quarters?"

"I think that some place more private than this would be more appropriate, Son. Colonel Hansen came along with me."

"I see," answered Alan, thinking it most unusual behavior. He saluted Troy and continued: "Good morning, Sir. Do you have a vehicle here?"

"The Maroon Wagoneer, Lieutenant," pointed Troy. "Why don't you drive it to your quarters? The key is in the ignition." Troy opened the passenger door for Gail and climbed in the back seat.

"That day I've been promising you for so many years has finally arrived, Alan."

"What do you mean, Mother?" asked Alan with a puzzled look on his face. He stopped the Wagoneer in front of a two story duplex in the Bachelor Quarters of the base. "Let's go inside. I'll put on a pot of coffee. Are you a coffee drinker, Colonel?"

"Did you ever see a soldier that wasn't?" he grinned.

The silence was awkward. They took a seat around the small kitchen table while Alan busied himself getting his coffee percolator going. He put a plate of fresh donuts in front of his guests and took a seat beside his mother opposite Troy waiting for the coffee to stop brewing.

Troy broke the tension first. "Why don't you go ahead, Gail? Start at the beginning when we first met in 1943."

Gail breathed deeply and began to tell Alan about their relationship on the hospital ship in the Mediterranean prior to the Normandy invasion. She left out nothing including their liaison the night they stayed together at that small inn on the Isle of Wright in the middle of May, 1944. Alan listened with singular attention. When she got to the part about being wounded in an artillery explosion, Gail began to cry.

"When I was wounded, my first worry was for my baby. God was with me that day, for you were born a healthy baby on February fifteenth, 1945. Figure it out for yourself. I believe Troy wants to say something to you," Gail cried, with tears flushing her eyes.

Troy sat erect in his chair and looked at Alan. "On our last meeting outside a USO Canteen center in England, your mother and I made a pact to meet one hundred and eighty days after the surrender of Germany at the prominent Wentworth-By-The-Sea Hotel in Newcastle, New Hampshire. As it turned out when my company was pulled from the line for rest, I went to look up your mother. Her unit was near the front then. Ninety percent of the medical battalion was destroyed during a

German artillery barrage. I was unable to find any record of her surviving the blast. I was out of my mind with grief. I kept our date at Wentworth-By-The-Sea and said good-bye to a memory.

"I had no way of knowing that she was alive until last month at the reunion tour. It was an unnerving discovery as you can imagine. So now, here we are informing you about your real father. What else can I say, Lieutenant? Your mother is the most courageous woman I've ever known. Her moral character is beyond reproach and worthy of profound respect. I wish that I could have been a part of your life, Alan. That was not possible and there's not much we can do about the past. The future is another matter and that rests in your hands."

"What about your family, Colonel?" asked Alan. He had absorbed every word they spoke without any exterior indication that he was surprised.

"I have two daughters. Cera was in Europe with me and you've already met her. My older daughter Karen lives in California. She's married and expecting a baby. I'll soon be a grandfather. My wife and I are going through a divorce that should be settled shortly. I've purchased a place in central Maine and plan to retire from the Army. It was less than twenty-four hours ago that I learned about my son. A West Point graduate automatically receives my respect and admiration. It's a little late for me to play the traditional father role, but I would like to extend the hand of friendship to you."

It was an emotionally powerful moment. The two soldiers sized each other up and embraced in a crushing bear hug. Tears flowed easily from both of them. Gail sat silently witnessing the bond that had just been established between the two soldiers in her life. She thanked God the meeting had gone so well. Tears continued to flow, but now they were tears of happiness and relief.

"It might come as a surprise to you, Mother, that when I met Colonel Hansen I had a feeling he was the soldier you told me about. Somehow it all fit together, especially your reaction to seeing him on the tour. Beyond that though, there was something unexplainable. I had a premonition about you and Cera when I met you. It was an awkward time to meet like strangers, yet I did not feel as if we were strangers."

161

"Now that I look back on it, Alan," Troy recalled, soberly. "There was something special about you that defied definition. I believe Cera felt the same way. You'll like her when you get to know her."

"Imagine, today I learn that I have a father and two half-sisters," exclaimed Alan, embracing his emotional mother. "As for you, Ma. Why were you so proud and independent? It should not have been necessary for you to carry the burden of raising a child alone."

"I've berated her about that very same thing, Alan. Your mother is a very special person. I can tell you that when I first met your mother and we became good friends, I loved her more than life itself. Now I hope that she will let me do my share. At this late date, you're a young man with a promising career ahead of him, but we can never have too many friends. I'd like to be included in that category."

"I promise to keep in touch and I'd like to seek your advice about Army affairs. Your record, as shown by the ribbons you wear, has been an extraordinary journey. I salute you, Colonel Hansen."

"Alan why don't we agree on what you're going to call Troy? Colonel or Mister Hansen is a little formal," Gail suggested, happy over the turn of events.

"I have no objections if you want to call me Troy or Father. Cera and Karen usually call me Dad or Daddy."

"If you don't object, I'll call you Father because that's who you are, and I've wanted to be able to call someone my father for a long time. It'll feel great to tell my friends and buddies that my father is a highly decorated soldier with combat experience in three wars. I'm glad that you turned out to be the man I've been searching for."

"So am I, Alan. What do you say if the three of us go out to celebrate this occasion at a good restaurant? As a matter of fact if my memory serves me correctly Fort Dix Officer's Club is one of the country's best."

"Sounds good to me," replied Alan, standing a little straighter and a little taller. Lack of knowledge of his birth father had left an empty place in his life. Now it was filled with expectations beyond his fondest dreams.

162

"That would be nice," added Gail, relieved of the terrible burden she had been carrying for all those years.

The officer's Club was busy. Dix was an important staging area and training center for the eastern part of the country. Alan was impressed at the way Troy was greeted by more senior officers that had served with him over the years. Respect and admiration is never a matter of course in the military. It had to be earned by performance.

During the meal, Alan asked his mother how Les was doing. She told him that Les was checking on her all the time. It was significant that Alan did not comment further about the policeman. Alan asked Troy about schools in the Army. He had some definite advice on that subject.

"Take every school course offered to you, Alan. Your West Point training may make the basic infantry course at Benning unnecessary, but try to get on the list for the advanced course just as soon as you can. You'll be surprised how much easier a company is to handle after taking the course. Also keep your eye open for command and staff schools at Leavenworth and Carlisle Barracks after you've made captain. If you don't have that on your resume, then chances are good that you may not go any higher than a major."

"I know that Ma will be pleased to learn that I'm going to Germany with the battalion. We're scheduled to do a series of training exercises with NATO countries for the next couple of years. It should be good duty." Alan squeezed his mother's hand.

"That's good news. I hated to think you might have returned to Vietnam."

They spent the balance of the day at Fort Dix touring around the base. Gail was a different person by the end of the day. She was experiencing how Troy and Alan had "connected" with each other, and it warmed her heart. Troy had promised to take Alan fishing on his next furlough, joking that he guarded the location of his favorite fish holes with vigor, but for Alan he'd make an exception.

Alan agreed to visit them at the Lake of Three Sorrows. Troy told him and Gail about the place and how much it meant to him. Gail was glad that he had found a peaceful sanctuary to call home. It sounded like an enchanting place.

At the end of the day, they left Alan at the reception center. Troy observed him in the rear view mirror standing straight and proud. "He's a fine young man, Gail. You've done a wonderful job with him." Troy saw her tears.

"He's always been a son that I was proud of," she admitted. "These tears are not sad ones. I leave Alan, for the first time, with a full understanding of who he is. I had denied him the knowledge of his complete identity and I was wrong. I'm sure he appreciates that. The two of you just made it all so easy."

"It was easy, Gail. I'm glad that it's behind us. Thanks for being so brave. No more regrets about the past okay? Let's rejoice that the future is going to be better and more complete. How serious are you and Les? If you think the question is out of bounds then I withdraw it."

"We've been good friends for a while. He likes to feel responsible for me. I can't tell you what I feel for him right now. I can honestly tell you that today has revived a lot of the old feelings I've pushed aside for a long time. I did what I did after the war because I loved you, Troy."

Her statement vibrated every nerve in his body. Last night after they had kissed, he had the feeling that things were happening all over again. He had never stopped loving her. This trip to see Alan was one of the best days he had in years. Just being near Gail made him feel complete. He had no right to expect anything more from her. For now he was content to know that she was doing well and he was satisfied with the knowledge of having a son in his life.

"What do you suggest? Shall we drive part way into Connecticut and put up again for the night?" asked Troy. It was beginning to get dark and he was honest about his ability to drive safely. "I could probably make it to your house, but I'd be stretching my ability to remain alert to the limit."

"Then we should do the prudent thing and stop wherever it looks like a good place to you. It has been an important day in our lives. Thank you for stepping up and being responsible about Alan. I expected that from you and now I regret not doing it sooner."

"I'm glad you insisted on coming along, Gail. Being with you and hearing your voice again has been important to me. Seeing those young recruits being formed into units at Dix has given me an opportunity to rethink my Army career. I've got some writing that I want to do. A friend of mine promised to use any essay I wanted to write about subjects I'm knowledgeable about, which of course is the Army. I don't want to retire to a rocking chair, but it will be nice to be in control of the time in my life. I confess, I'm reserving a portion of my life strictly for fishing. Alan and I can enjoy that together. I can hardly wait for his leave time."

Gail touched his face with her fingers feeling his nose and eyes without blocking his view of the road. He took her fingers and kissed them.

"I've grown older just like everyone else."

"I remember how you looked. You show maturity well, Troy. You and Alan have very similar bone structure. That means that he's a handsome man too."

"Your generous praise is going to give me a big head," chuckled Troy. She smiled with him.

Two hours from Fort Dix Troy stopped at a motel with a large restaurant and paid for two single rooms side by side. They went into the restaurant for light refreshment. Troy ordered a cup of coffee and a piece of fresh custard pie. Gail ordered apple pie a la mode with her coffee and ate the pie with a spoon.

"If I'm not careful on this trip, I'll gain weight," Gail giggled.

At times, Troy saw some of the same playful mannerisms in Gail that he had noticed years ago. The way she had tilted her head slightly to the right when she laughed had not changed. A reflective period of silence between them gave each a chance to evaluate what it meant to be together again. The restaurant was playing a series of slow golden oldies as background music. They heard the plaintive refrain of *White Cliffs of Dover* and *I'll Be Seeing You*, by Vera Lynn. Gail listened to the music with an enlightened degree of perception unique to the blind.

"Those were frightening times for me, yet for a moment in the midst of chaos, we were able to forget the war and its horrors. It was an interlude that strengthened me for a long time," Gail reflected solemnly.

"I never forgot that time. I probably would have gone crazy without your encouragement. It was a long hard war. Korea and Vietnam were easier for me to handle. Was it hard for you to give up nursing, Gail?" Troy asked, remembering how the patients in her wards idolized her and how kind and generous she was with them.

"Yes, I cried for days because it was no longer available for me. It's one of the jobs in which a blind person could be a risk to the patients. I could have worked in physical therapy but declined. Teaching has been rewarding for me. The students have been great, I make each class responsible for my safety and limitations. You'd be surprised how well they mature and accept that responsibility. I was pleased to learn that I had some of the most accomplished classes in the high school for the past fifteen years."

"I'm not surprised, the Army gets those same young people after they graduate from high school. We put a uniform with a code of excellence on them and they never fail to make us proud," Troy added, paying the bill.

He escorted Gail back to the rooms. It felt good to have her on his arm. "Here we are, Gail. Sleep well. Thanks for making this a very special day for me."

"It is I who must thank you for being yourself," she clung to his arm and ran her fingers across his face. "If you want to share one room, I will not say no."

"I want that more than you know, Gail. As of this minute, I'm still a married man and you're engaged to Les. I think it's for the best not to violate that trust. Goodnight, Gail."

"Goodnight, Troy," she said, lifting her lips to him. "You know what's happening again don't you?"

"Yes..."

Chapter Twenty

By noon the next day Troy was at Gail's house in Amesbury. They had stopped at a grocery store near her home for fresh bread and milk. Troy escorted her to the porch of the house where she insisted on opening up the house without assistance. He placed her suitcase on the porch and retrieved two grocery bags from the Wagoneer, carrying them into the kitchen. Gail offered to make sandwiches and coffee for lunch. As she was preparing them she heard a police car stop in the driveway. The sound of the automobile was familiar to her.

"Here comes Les," said Gail with a sigh.

Troy did not know how to interpret her unenthusiastic response. Les knocked on the door and let himself in without waiting for an invitation. Troy turned to confront the officer who was trying to hide a burning rage in his penetrating dark eyes.

"I was concerned for you, Gail," stammered Les in an effort to sound casual. He looked Troy up and down in his lightweight summer tan uniform. "You could have called to let me know that you were safe."

"She was with me, Sergeant Aiken, and I'm capable of looking after her safety. Your concern is appreciated but was not really necessary." Troy defended his actions.

"Les, this is neither the time nor place for a scene. We were just going to have lunch. Would you like to join us in a ham and cheese sandwich?" offered Gail with a nervous tremor in her voice. "I'm a mature woman and I don't need to check in with you or anyone else about my decisions to do things as I please."

"I've already eaten," Les snapped back at her. "It doesn't look good when a man's fiancée leaves for two nights with an old friend. A good friend wouldn't do such a thing." Les was even more upset by the indifferent attitude he was facing in the kitchen.

"If Gail was my fiancée I would not embarrass her the way you're doing right now," Troy stated in a calm voice, looking directly at Les.

"Who are you to talk like that to me?" warned Les. He turned to leave the room nudging Troy out of the way with his left arm, catching Troy off balance. Troy grabbed the edge of the kitchen table for support. Gail felt the table move from the sudden pressure against it. "Get out of my way, doggie," Les growled in anger. It was a derogatory title that marines frequently applied to soldiers.

Troy resented the slur. Without warning he grasped Les by his left arm spinning him around so that they were facing each other. Troy then hit him with both hands using sharp Karate chops to the base of Les's neck. His knees buckled, but Troy held him upright against the door jamb.

"Don't forget jarhead, some doggies bite. I'd like to hear an apology from you to the lady of the house. Your brutish behavior is out of line and uncalled for." Troy remained calm.

Infuriated by the way Troy had temporarily disabled him, Les, apologized and left the house, slightly unsteady, in a more humble mood than he entered. Troy followed him to the porch where he made several barking sounds before returning to the kitchen where Gail was cradling her head on the table, crying.

"I apologize for adding to the bad scene, Gail. I could never stand it when marines puffed up with self-importance insulted me or any of my soldiers. Maybe Les will think twice the next time he's tempted. I should have swallowed my pride and let him mouth off and leave."

"I'd say that you handled the situation with a proper response, Troy. Les was just plain wrong! I've never seen him like this. I knew that he had a temper but it was always under control around me."

"I expect that tomorrow he'll be back with hat in hand seeking an apology. His anger was directed at me not you. Are you still hungry?" asked Troy, trying to make light of the situation.

"I was before we got interrupted," she admitted, wiping the tears from her eyes.

Troy had a ham and cheese sandwich with her. He watched her measure out the coffee and water for the coffee maker with precise movements using a finger to feel over the edge of the pot to measure the water level. She then placed two full scoops of coffee in the filter bowl before turning the machine on. They finished the meal with a jelly donut each. Troy could not pass them up at the grocery store. He checked his watch and told her that he was going to stop at Togus for a checkup before returning to the Lake of Three Sorrows.

"This trip has changed my life, Gail," he said seriously. "I'd like to leave you with a few thoughts. If there is ever a time when you need me for any purpose, please promise to call. I will always be there for you. Would you sit down at your Braille typewriter and type my phone number and address? That way you'll have it in case you need it."

"All right," she said, sitting down at the counter in front of her large typewriter. She typed the address and phone number as he dictated and then read them back to him:

"Route #2, Box Number 180, Kokadjo, Maine. Telephone number 1-104-487-5551."

"That's correct. Who'll read my letters for you if I write?" asked Troy.

"I have a dear friend next door. There are no secrets between us. Whatever is read or said in her presence, stays here. I trust her completely," replied Gail.

"I like that. Good-bye, Gail. These past two days have been an amazing revelation for me. Just being with you has made them special. I'll keep in touch."

"Good-bye, Troy," she said, putting her arm around his waist, walking with him to the porch. "My thoughts go with you. Thanks for accepting Alan so well."

"I intend to be a part of his life from now on. I wish you happiness and fulfillment of all your dreams, Gail. Good-bye." He held her in a warm embrace for a long time. Gail lifted her lips to him.

"Gail…"

"Not now, Troy, I want to remember this moment. Please leave and don't look back because I know I'm going to cry."

Troy reluctantly got behind the wheel of the Wagoneer. She stood in the screen porch door following the sound of the Wagoneer's engine as he drove away. Tears rolled beneath her glasses. She stared into her special world of darkness for a long time and slowly returned to the kitchen where she picked up the sheet of paper from the typewriter and read Troy's address with her supple fingers.

Later that same night, the headlights from the Wagoneer flashed across the cabin at the Lake of Three Sorrows. The kitchen light was on. Cera saw the lights reflect on the porch where she was sitting on the swing listening to the sounds of the evening. She ran to hug her father before he could speak.

"Welcome home, Daddy. I've been worried about you these past two days. How was the trip? Tell me the truth now. I knew a lot of things before you did. I made a vow of silence to Gail. She wanted to do that herself," said Cera, anxious to hear what he had to say.

"She did that all right, Cera," he replied. It was nice to be welcomed home with such enthusiasm. "Gail went with me to Fort Dix where we had an interesting visit with Alan. Once she told me about Alan it made everything easier to understand. I'm not upset or angry. To the contrary, I'm going to enjoy being a father to Alan, too. What do you really think about it, Cera? Are you disappointed with your old dad or think less about me for what Gail and I had twenty-five years ago? I've been thinking of you and Karen all the way back to Maine." Troy placed his suitcase on the porch and sat on the swing, glad to be home.

"I was angry when Gail first told me. I don't know why, I suppose I had romantic notions that you and mom went from the innocence of youth to adulthood without anyone else in between. I've grown up a lot this summer. I can't judge you and Gail. I've never been as frightened as the two of you must have been during the war. It was a real commitment on your part, Daddy, because you've carried her memory without sharing it with anybody, even Mother."

"It had nothing to do with your mother."

170

"I know that now, Daddy. That first time when I saw you look at Gail in England, I knew what was in your heart. I pray that I may have that same kind of love for a man. Don't apologize for having the feelings. I admire you for nurturing them for so long."

"I love you, daughter. Gail was impressed with you," Troy said, watching her gently rock in and out of a light beam from the kitchen. This summer she had blossomed into a beautiful young lady. He had a feeling that a courageous helicopter pilot by the name of John Lamprey might have something to do with the glow of happiness he saw on her face. "How's John doing? I stopped at Togus on my way. He was in a therapy session so I came along without seeing him. The doctors say that he's doing extraordinarily well. They told me that you could be the inspiration behind his progress. Is that true?"

"I suppose so," she answered shyly. "His will to be as normal as his injuries permit is phenomenal. I'm pleased if I've helped him. The fact is, he's inspired me with his quiet courage."

"I'm glad for you, Honey. I like John a lot. I've had glimpses of his determination. It was not difficult to imagine him doing what the citation for the Medal of Honor proclaims. He's a true hero in every sense of the word."

"Sometimes he pushes too hard," cried Cera impatiently.

"How is that?"

"He's already checking into the requirements necessary for certification as a civilian helicopter pilot. He honestly believes that he can surpass the requirements. He could be killed!"

"Don't deny him the opportunity to prove that he will be as good as he was before being wounded. There's a lot more to it than simply wanting to fly."

"I don't want to discourage him. That's the last thing I want to do. Still, the thought of him behind the controls of a helicopter frightens me," Cera said firmly.

"Don't forget that the last time he flew, he evacuated his comrades while the enemy was trying hard to kill all of them. That won't be happening to him in Maine. Flying a helicopter under civilian conditions will be a cinch compared to flying in combat."

"You're right, Daddy, as usual," answered Cera, shrugging her shoulders.

John and Cera continued to see each other throughout the summer. He was released from Togus in mid-August. Cera brought him home in the Wagoneer. He asked her if he could drive it, promising that he would relinquish the wheel if he was unable to safely control the vehicle. She complied, with some misgivings, because she did not want him to try things too quickly and get disappointed with premature failure. At first it felt awkward to him, but he soon developed positions and movements that bolstered his confidence and ease behind the wheel. After a few miles he turned into a roadside rest area on Route 95. He turned to look at Cera with a nervous anxiety and reached in his pocket.

"I have something I'd like to give to you, Cera," he announced with a shaky voice.

"What is it, John?"

"This is an engagement ring that belonged to my grandmother and my mother. I'd be honored if you would accept it as a commitment to our future."

"Are you proposing to me, John?"

"Yes," he said nervously. "It's true we hardly know each other, but from what I've already seen I want to share my life with you. I love you, Cera."

Cera began to cry. She had been having similar thoughts lately. The idea of returning to school in September meant that she would be that much further away from him. She had been a part of his progress from an angry morose patient to a high-spirited fighter ready to take on the world. It had been a wonderful adventure.

"I accept your proposal, John. We do need time to plan our future and get better acquainted. I'll be proud to be your betrothed," Cera answered, kissing him warmly.

"I haven't told you yet, but the high school where I taught has offered me a part time job as a substitute teacher. That way I'll be able to work into it on a less demanding schedule, and when I think I'm ready, they promised me my old position back," John announced proudly.

"You continue to amaze me, John Lamprey!"

Two weeks later, he passed his helicopter test and was issued a license, renewable every year!

The warm days of summer passed quickly. The summer solstice in June marked the high mark for the season. Each succeeding day became shorter by several minutes. Troy took early retirement from the Army. Doctors at Togus told him that he had recovered as far as it was possible. However, it was not enough to meet the standards they had to apply to all Army officers. They gave him a medical discharge and commensurate disability pension. By the end of the summer he had conditioned his body to his normal weight and muscle tone. When he was twenty-four years old he had earned a black belt in Karate and had maintained a high level of excellence over the years. By the end of the summer he again qualified for the black belt. He was prepared to take on the world on his terms as a retiree.

The lawyers for Beth and Troy completed their divorce proceedings along the lines of what they originally agreed. Troy received the papers requiring his signature late in August. He had mixed feelings. No matter how one looked upon the dissolution of a marriage, it was a failure, and Troy always took failure seriously.

Troy had received a letter from Gail a few days after their trip to Fort Dix. She told him that her relationship with Les was strained as a result of their being together on the trip to see Alan. Evidently he had a need to control her life more than she wanted him to dictate her every move. It was destined to wither on the vine. He spoke occasionally to her over the phone and planned for his next trip down to see her.

The trip had to be postponed because Troy came down with a debilitating flu that kept him in bed for several days. He developed a fever of 103 degrees when Cera called a doctor for him. There was little to be done except to administer aspirin to control pain and cold packs to bring the fever down. Gail called on the day when his fever was at its peak. Cera answered the phone.

"Hello."

"Hello, Cera. This is Gail. Is your father at home?"

"Yes he is, Gail, but he's sick with the flu. The doctor has him on aspirins and antibiotics. He's resting right now. His fever has been making him weak and lethargic."

"Oh, that's too bad. Tell him that I called. You want to be careful not to overextend yourself Cera while caring for your father. I heard from Alan today. He's still in Germany with NATO. He sends his regards to all of you. I'm so glad that I don't have to hide the truth from him anymore. Your father was wonderful with Alan."

"My Father is wonderful with everybody, Gail. He's been doing well this summer. He's stronger emotionally and physically than he was when we first arrived in Maine. Much of that progress I attribute to you, Gail. He never says anything, he's inclined to keep his thoughts to himself, but I'm positive that he thinks of you often. He talks about you a lot. He especially remembers how you cared for the wounded men in your ward."

"That was a long time ago, young lady. Things change."

"Do they?" asked Cera directly.

"Please Cera, let's not go where you're heading. I'm not the person I was..."

Cera heard the words. They were words of denial and regret. "Gail may I ask you something?"

"If you wish, Cera."

"If you had a chance, would you like to come here for a visit at the Lake of Three Sorrows while Dad is recuperating from the flu?"

"Yes, I would. I'm worried about him."

"All right, Gail. I'll call you in a while to let you know," assured Cera.

"Thank you, Cera, I appreciate your kindness," Gail replied.

The day after Cera spoke to Gail, she was fixing a light breakfast of poached egg on toast for Troy. His fever had broken and his appetite was picking up. She placed the tray on his bed stand when the sound of helicopter rotors filled the cabin. The second he heard the rotors it brought him back to Vietnam. He tensed and remembered how it was over there.

Cera saw the reaction and hugged him. The ugly memories disappeared as quickly as they came.

"It's all right, Daddy. It's a surprise for you, it's John. He has passed his licensing procedures. The helicopter belongs to a flying club in Bangor. Club members can rent it on a daily basis. I rode in it with John at the controls the last time I went to see him. He's been anxious to see the place from the air."

Cera ran out the back door to the large bedrock outcrop at the rear of the cabin. John was tethering the machine to nearby trees. She ran to hug John and turned excitedly to his passenger, Gail.

"Welcome to the Lake Of Three Sorrows, Gail. How was your flight?"

"Your fiancé made my first helicopter ride a joy. You marry that young man, Cera, he's one of the rare ones."

"I think so too," Cera answered, embracing the intrepid blind lady. John finished anchoring the craft and carried Gail's suitcase. He was agile and confident in his moves on the rough rocky surface.

"You handled the machine so smoothly that I did not have a chance to be afraid. Thank you, John. He picked me up at a golf course across the street from my house," Gail explained, excited and flushed at being the center of attention.

The sun was warm with a soft breeze from the northeast sweeping the canopies of spruce and pine, filling the air with the enduring scent of the northern forest.

"My, my, the air is so sweet and fresh," remarked Gail, breathing deeply. "I can hear the wind blowing through the trees. This place is filled with serenity. Your father called it his sanctuary. I understand now what he meant."

"He doesn't know that you're coming, Gail. It'll be a pleasant surprise. This morning I believe you're just what the doctor ordered for him," said Cera, guiding her towards the cabin.

"You're such a generous and giving girl, Cera. Thank you for your thoughtfulness."

"And you, dear lady, are everything my father has told me and then some. We're coming to a set of steps now, the back door of the cabin. Father is in a room on your left. I'll walk you to the door. There's no sill on the door so don't worry about stubbing your foot on it," Cera whispered in her ear. "Go through the door and turn left. His bed is against the same wall. When you go through the door and pivot left, you're only five feet from him. John and I are going to sit out on the porch. Would you like a cup of coffee?"

Gail shook her head in the affirmative. She was enjoying the prospect of surprising Troy. He was sitting up in bed drinking orange juice. He heard a board squeak and looked up expecting to see John and Cera. Gail stood before him dressed in a light blue dress with lace covering her neck. Her hair was pulled to the top of her head and held in place with two red barrettes. She was a vision of loveliness and his heart pounded wildly.

"Gail," he uttered in disbelief. "Come and sit beside me. The bed is two feet in front of you." He held a hand towards her. She approached him confidently, touched the bed and upon finding his hand grasped it and held on tight.

"I just had my first helicopter ride, Troy," she exclaimed. "Cera told me that you were sick and I wanted to come. How are you doing?" She sat on the bed and ran her hands over his forehead and through his hair. Her soft touch sent ripples through his body.

"It's nice to see you again, Gail," he confessed, holding her hands.

"How could I stay away knowing that you're sick?" It was a simple statement that spoke volumes to him. "You still have a slight fever. What have you been eating?"

"Cera made me poached egg and toast. It tasted good. I haven't eaten for a couple of days. I just finished a glass of orange juice too."

"That's a good start."

Cera and John entered the room to announce that they were going to take a ride down to Moosehead Lake and take a look at Kineo Island from the air.

"Congratulations on your being certified to fly again, John. Right now I'm not sure if it's the joy of flying or my lovely daughter that puts the sparkle you have in your eyes," Troy smiled at him.

John blushed. "Probably both, Sir. This morning I picked up Gail almost from her doorstep. I made fuel stops in Portland and Greenville before coming here. She was a model passenger. She fed me peanut butter and jelly sandwiches while I handled the controls. She can ride with me any time and place," John told them, patting her on the shoulder. The two severely wounded veterans had already built a common bond of fellowship, valued by each of them.

"It was a wonderful experience, John. I admire your ability to rise above your limitations. I know how much discipline it takes. I hate it when people look upon you and I as cripples. We're simply disabled and I've found that most people have some form of disability. If it's not physical it's emotional or spiritual, but a disability nevertheless."

"I've never heard it put that way," answered John with a knowing smile. "Your spirit is contagious and an inspiration to all of us."

"Could I show you around the cabin before John and I leave?" asked Cera.

"Please do," replied Gail, accepting Cera's arm. "The air here is so fresh and sweet smelling. There's something about this cabin that makes me feel at ease. Peace and harmony wreaks from its walls."

"I believe you've already been captivated by its gentle enchantment, Gail. Dad and I have felt the same thing."

Cera walked Gail through the bathroom patiently allowing her time to study the orientation of its contents. The great room was a combination kitchen, dining room, and living room. They began with a sweep around the four walls beginning with the large fireplace and bookshelves on the north wall. The guest bedroom was next to Troy's room. They spent several minutes there while Gail located the bed, closet, and windows. Once she had a mental image of the room she was able to lock it into her memory.

Each room and piece of furniture was catalogued as it related to the rest of the cabin. She created a mosaic of the floor plan and memorized it. Everything became a small part of a larger master plan. Gail began to develop the skill shortly after her blindness. She filled in the voids of what was around her with sound, scent and touch distinguishing texture and density of objects. They continued around to the ladder leading to the loft above.

"I sleep in the loft," Cera told her. "I love it up there, it makes me feel warm and secure."

"I'm sure, my dear. This cabin is charming," Gail replied. She brushed her hand across the ladder to the loft. It fell on a smooth glossy surface. She became excited and ran her hand to the cover of the keyboard. "Oh, my Lord, you have a piano."

"Do you play," asked Cera.

"Yes, I've always had a piano at my home. Two years ago it was broken and destroyed when the house was burglarized. I've missed not being able to play. May I try it?"

"Please do, Gail. All I can do is chopsticks on it," laughed Cera.

Gail sat erect at the bench unfolding the cover from the keyboard. Positioning her fingers on the keys she ran up and down the scale two or three times. A soft look of contentment came over her face. She began a medley of popular songs of the day: *Mrs. Robinson, Ballad Of The Green Berets, Moon River, Born Free* and ended with portions of three songs that were part of an era she and Troy recalled so vividly, *I'll Be Seeing You In All The Old Familiar Places, Paper Doll* and *The White Cliffs Of Dover*.

When she stopped, claps and whistles came from the bedroom where Troy and John listened with rapt attention as the cabin filled with music. Gail smiled all over. She was happy!

"I've missed not being able to play."

"That was beautiful," said Cera, impressed with the feeling the blind lady gave to the music. "You play very well."

As soon as John and Cera lifted off the bedrock ledge, Gail once again familiarized herself with the kitchen area. She found the coffee pot and tin of coffee with a measuring spoon. She found the coffee mugs and used one to pre-measure the water for two cups of coffee. The coffee pot had two dials. Gail retraced her steps to Troy's room.

"What about the two dials on the coffee pot?" she asked.

"The one on the left is for strength. Turn the dial straight up and down. The one on the right is an off and on switch. Turn it to the right for on and to the left for off. There's a point midway on it for automatic settings. I never use that. It's too complicated," Troy chuckled. "I have a feeling that you're as much of a coffee addict as I am. It's nice to have you here, Gail. I'm sorry I'm not feeling up to par, but I'm stronger than I was yesterday."

"I'll turn the coffee on and be right in," she said. Her mental map of the cabin was slowly being supplemented. The range and counter top was seven single steps from the door to Troy's room. She retraced her steps with confidence.

"Your ability to adapt is amazing," Troy observed, settling against a fresh pillow Gail placed beneath his head.

"I'm glad to have a chance to talk in private with you Troy," she announced in a serious tone. "The school board has asked me to come back for another year if I want the job. I've got to make a decision shortly. Ever since the trip you and I took to Fort Dix my life has been in complete disarray. Les has voluntarily stepped out of my life. I think he was afraid of you."

"I apologize if I was too harsh with him. He asked for what he got."

"I'm sure you're right, Troy. He was more interested in controlling me than he was trying to make me happy. We really had little in common. He's gone and I'm relieved about the situation. Now that we're alone, where do we go from here, Troy? Time at our age is so fleeting. I want to tell you that I fell in love with you during the war and it's just as strong now as it was then. Having said that, I'm aware more than anybody else that my blindness can be a burden. I have no delusions about that. Have you given any thought of what's next?"

"Just about every minute of the day! Will you marry me, Gail? I know now that my life will never be complete unless I can share it with you. I need you more than you'll ever know. I've prayed that someday I'd be able to call you my wife."

Tears streamed down Gail's cheeks. "I was hoping that I'd hear you say that, Troy. I didn't know for certain unless I asked. Let's make it soon. I don't want to lose any more time and, please, don't ever say good-bye to me again. My world collapses when you're not with me. I love you."

Chapter Twenty-One

One Year Later, summer, 1971

A family celebration of thanksgiving was being planned at the Lake of Three Sorrows. A gathering of the clan for the first time since Troy and Gail were married August 30, 1970. John Lamprey and Cera were frequent visitors on holidays and weekends when their schedules permitted. John was teaching at his old high school. Cera had one more year to go at the University of New Hampshire. Shortly after graduation, she and John planned to get married. Their love for each other continued to grow with each passing day. It was a relationship that pleased Troy. The two young people complimented each other.

From the first day they were married, Gail took her place as the lady of the house ruling her domain with love and grace. She gave the cabin and it's environs her characteristic attention to order. Their happiness together was a topic of conversation by everyone who experienced the deep commitment that motivated them. The cabin was a model of harmony and serenity. The absence of chaos and discord was felt by all.

One day, shortly after they were married, Troy brought home a bundle of soft fur and energy in the form of a fox terrier puppy for Gail. He was white and brown with splashes of black. His ears stood up straight except for the top one third which flopped forward. The puppy took to Gail right off. She called him Noodles because he liked left-over spaghetti. Most of the time he was at her side. At nighttime he slept on the floor beside the bed. No matter where she was sitting on the porch or in the great- room, Noodles would announce his presence by laying his head on her lap for a few seconds. It was almost as if he sensed her limitations and took it upon himself to be her protector. He became an important member of the family. His loyalty to Gail had earned a place in their hearts.

One day late in June, Ashley Cooper called Troy to ask if she could visit for a while. She had been ill and had to give up her nursing position at the village infirmary.

"You'll never need to ask for permission, Ashley. You're welcome at anytime, and I mean that sincerely. Would you like Gail and I to drive up to get you?"

"I sold my Jeep last winter," she said in a weak voice. "I'd hate to put you out."

"Listen, Ashley, I would not have offered it if I didn't mean it. Gail and I are planning a family gathering sometime this summer. Having you here with us will make it special. I have no doubt that you'll love Gail and she'll love you in return. You two have a lot in common, dear lady. We'll leave tomorrow morning and be there day after tomorrow. Don't worry, we have your address and will find you."

"Thank you, dear friend. I'm so anxious to go back to the only home I've ever known," Ashley said in a faltering voice.

"You gather your things, Ashley, and we'll be there. It will be nice to welcome you back home for as long as you want. Give us a chance to show you how much you mean to us."

"Thank you, Troy," the lovely Indian lady replied. Tears of happiness filled her sad eyes. "I've treasured the letters that Gail has typed to me. The goodness in her heart is expressed in her words. I'm glad for both of you. The cabin has a history of cultivating wellness and a sense of security."

"You're right, Ashley. You take care of yourself and we'll be there before you know it."

"Good-bye, Troy and thank you."

By the time Troy and Gail returned to the cabin with Ashley, the two ladies had become friends and enjoyed each other's company. They were both trained nurses from an era that established their tradition of excellence. Troy thought that she had failed some since she sold the cabin to him. He and Gail moved out of the original bedroom Ashley and Dale had shared, and moved into a new room addition they had recently completed.

Karen and Ken had flown into Bangor and rented a car for the trip to the cabin. They brought with them Troy's six month old granddaughter, Charissa. The little girl soon ruled the household and was the center of attention. Ashley and Gail took her into their hearts and took turns changing diapers and feeding her. Troy used his position as patriarch of the family to not do diapers but he did enjoy feeding Charissa her bottle and expertly burped her.

Ashley readily assimilated into the routines of Gail and Troy. The cabin was filled with memories and she was content being with good friends. She and Gail played piano duets a lot together. Laughter filled the cabin when they were sitting side by side on the bench accompanying each other's selections. Their versatility was tested by many of the classics they preferred. They joked about their mistakes and played with enthusiasm. It tickled Troy to hear them going at it.

John and Cera had flown in from Durham in the helicopter John rented from his club. Alan arrived at the same time in a taxi from Greenville. He had flown from Germany directly to Montreal where he boarded a Canadian Pacific train for Greenville.

Troy had fabricated a large tavern type table set up on the front porch. It was large enough to accommodate eight people. The table was heavily laden with succulent steaks, chops, salads, and a variety of drinks and vegetables and fruits. Ashley had made several of her Swedish boulla breads she had inherited from Dale for the occasion. Troy and Gail were already addicted to them in the short time she had been with them.

Everybody gathered around the table. Ashley and Gail sat at either end. Troy stood after everyone was seated. He looked at each person around the table, his heart filled with pride and thanksgiving. He said a short prayer asking for God's blessing on the gathering and sat down. Alan slowly rose and cleared his throat.

"I want to express my appreciation and admiration for what the members around this beautifully stocked table represents, a family. I grew up with a mother that was special in every way that defines mothers. I was happy in that small world of the two of us, because she made it that way. Now that I've discovered the joy and warmth of a larger circle of family members words to describe the feeling escapes me at this moment. For myself and my dear mother, I want to say thank you for opening your hearts to us. I propose a toast for the celebration of life and a commitment to embrace the future."

Ashley stood up and spoke in her silvery voice. Everyone listened carefully, for her voice was not as strong as it used to be. "My dear friends, I have returned to this cabin on the Lake of Three Sorrows because it is here that I really began to live. I was a young girl about Cera's age when I first experienced its healing powers. The world has turned over many times since that day and its magical enchantment still touches my heart. To be a part of a family again is the answer to all my hopes and dreams. Thank you all for making it possible." She reached up with a long thin finger and wiped a tear from her left eye and sat down.

That night the heavens opened up with a burst of exotic lights from the aurora borealis. The sky was filled with lines of bright colors darting across the blue voids of the night. Red, yellow and orange merged and pulled away in erratic designs of color and electronic imagery. The loons called from the ends of the lake filling the still air with their sad melancholic calls the same way they had been doing for ages long past. The night was one that everybody remembered over the years. The fellowship and bonding of a family unit were strongly established on the banks of the Lake of Three Sorrows. Late that same evening everybody heard the soft melodious voice of the Indian Maiden blow across the lake. She was singing the haunting refrain of an ancient lullaby mourning the death of her two children.

The End

Other Historical Romance Novels
BY
Clifton LaBree

A Song for Lisa   A Historical Romance

This is the story of a young American woman captured by the Japanese in the Philippines, 1941. Like most prisoners, she was brutalized and sadistically treated with a cruel disregard for human life. Three years later, Lisa and her companions had reached the low point of starvation and abuse .....

Lake of Three Sorrows   A Historical Romance

A warm spiritually uplifting story of courage, commitment, and sacrifice. This is the story of Dale Cooper, a battle-weary American soldier who served in two world wars.

Flickering Flame (Colonial Series Book One)

A historical novel, about the Cullen family who settled in Portsmouth, New Hampshire, and their participation in events prior to the French and Indian War. Freedom and opportunity were on the march, but it extracted a heavy price. Frontier settlers were ruthlessly killed and butchered by rampaging Indians lead by French officers and Jesuit priests who frequently incited them to greater levels of inhumanity...

Raising the Torch (Colonial Series Book Two)

A continuation of the saga from Flickering Flame, Colonial Series book one, of the Cullen family in Colonial Portsmouth. This is a moving story of love and sacrifice when a small colony had the audacity to fight for independence from their motherland...

Non-Fiction Books

By

Clifton LaBree

New Hampshire's General John Stark, Live Free or Die: Death Is Not the Greatest of Evils

Publisher - Fading Shadows Imprint

A fresh look at one of America's staunchest defenders of liberty and freedom. John Stark was a courageous New Hampshire citizen-soldier who fought in both, the French and Indian War, and the Revolutionary War. His pursuit of leadership excellence on the battlefield distinguished him as one of the most successful combat commanders of the war, and one of the least appreciated.

His selflessness, modest life style, and devotion to the cause of freedom are an inspiration that time has not diminished. He remains today the embodiment of the frugal, independent, and cantankerous New Hampshire Yankee.

Gentle Warrior, General Oliver Prince Smith, USMC

Published by - Kent State University Press. Kent, Ohio, 2001

The Story of one of the United States Marine Corps best General Officer. His flawless performance in Korea is a story that needed to be told.

FADING SHADOWS IMPRINT

Fading Shadows Imprint was established to bring to the public books of historical events and portraits of people enduring tragic circumstances of by-gone days. Hopefully, they will generate a deep appreciation and respect for the exceptionalness of the United States of America, and an appreciation for the sacrifice and selflessness of those who valiantly served for liberty and freedom.

The characters are fictional, but the historical events and dates have been seriously researched and are factually presented. Some books feature incidents during the French and Indian Wars as well as the War for Independence.

World Wars I and II are eras rich in stories that beg to be told. I've tried to pay tribute to the collective courage and heroism, often unheralded, that has defined Americans in every engagement. It was a time when the immortality of dreams and aspirations were defended by the blood of young men and women. There is a beautiful monument and cemetery in a small French village where thousands of white crosses and Stars-of-David are set in perfect alignment, honoring thousands of American soldiers who gave their last full measure. A large granite slab bearing mute witness to their sacrifice has the following words chiseled in stone: TIME WILL NOT DIM THE GLORY OF THEIR DEEDS. Another monument reads: VIRTUE AND COURAGE ARE THEIR OWN MONUMENT AND REWARD. Those simple words define the American soldier from the dark days of the Revolutionary War to the present. They are an American treasure, unique in the history of the world.

Every generation has its own signature and characteristics that uniquely define them. The World War II generation is defined by the immortality of the ideals and truth they gallantly defended.

The United States has freely given precious blood and treasure to defend the rights of man to be free, and we have never asked for anything in return. No other nation on the planet has sacrificed so much for the noble virtues of liberty and freedom. We hope that the selections offered by Fading Shadows Imprint will touch your hearts and generate a deeper appreciation and love for our country.

www.ingramcontent.com/pod-product-compliance
Lightning Source LLC
Chambersburg PA
CBHW072136170626
46813CB00004BA/1587